Peng

Soldier Boy

 ANTHONY HILL is a Canberra-based author of books for children and adults. Born in Melbourne in 1942, he became a newspaper journalist before moving with his family to a small country town in New South Wales where they ran an antique shop. The experience formed the basis of his first two books, *The Bunburyists* and *Antique Furniture in Australia*.

Anthony Hill's first book for children, *Birdsong*, was published in 1988, followed in 1994 by his award-winning novella *The Burnt Stick*, illustrated by Mark Sofilas. The two combined again to produce *Spindrift* in 1996.

For ten years Anthony Hill was a speech writer for the Governor-General, until his recent retirement to concentrate full time on his writing. His own travels to the Gallipoli peninsula and the battlefields of the Great War underscore much of his writing in *Soldier Boy*.

Winner of the 2002 NSW Premier's Literary Awards (Ethel Turner Prize) and Honour Book in the 2002 Children's Book Council of Australia Book of the Year Awards (Eve Pownall Award for Information Books).

'This book is a model of historical writing for young (and old) readers . . . a significant contribution to the nation's culture . . .' (*Judge's report*)

ALSO BY ANTHONY HILL

The Bunburyists
Antique Furniture in Australia
Birdsong
The Burnt Stick
Spindrift
The Grandfather Clock
Growing Up and Other Stories
Forbidden
Young Digger
The Shadow Dog
Animal Heroes
Harriet
Captain Cook's Apprentice

Soldier Boy

THE TRUE STORY OF JIM MARTIN
THE YOUNGEST ANZAC

ANTHONY HILL

Anthony Hill
2013.

Penguin Books

PENGUIN BOOKS

Published by the Penguin Group
Penguin Group (Australia)
250 Camberwell Road, Camberwell, Victoria 3124, Australia
(a division of Pearson Australia Group Pty Ltd)
Penguin Group (USA) Inc.
375 Hudson Street, New York, New York 10014, USA
Penguin Group (Canada)
90 Eglinton Avenue East, Suite 700, Toronto ON M4P 2Y3, Canada
(a division of Pearson Penguin Canada Inc.)
Penguin Books Ltd
80 Strand, London WC2R 0RL, England
Penguin Ireland
25 St Stephen's Green, Dublin 2, Ireland
(a division of Penguin Books Ltd)
Penguin Books India Pvt Ltd
11, Community Centre, Panchsheel Park, New Delhi-110 017, India
Penguin Group (NZ)
67 Apollo Drive, Rosedale, North Shore 0632, New Zealand
(a division of Pearson New Zealand Ltd)
Penguin Books (South Africa) (Pty) Ltd
24 Sturdee Avenue, Rosebank, Johannesburg 2196, South Africa

Penguin Books Ltd, Registered Offices: 80 Strand, London WC2R 0RL, England

First published by Penguin Books Australia, 2001

25 24 23 22 21 20 19

Designed by Cathy Larsen, Penguin Design Studio
Maps drawn by Pat Kermode
Typeset in 11.5/16pt Bembo by Midland Typesetters, Maryborough, Victoria
Printed in Australia by McPherson's Printing Group, Maryborough, Victoria

National Library of Australia
Cataloguing-in-Publication data:

Hill, Anthony, 1942– .
    Soldier boy: the true story of Jim Martin, the youngest Anzac.
    (pbk.).

    Bibliography.
    ISBN 978 0 14 100330 6

    1. Martin, Jim, d. 1915. 2. World War, 1914–1918 – Australia – Biography.
    3. World War, 1914–1918 – Campaigns – Turkey – Gallipoli Peninsula – Biography.
    I. Title.

940.426

penguin.com.au

The author wishes to express particular thanks to his publisher Julie Watts and editor
Suzanne Wilson for the care and understanding they have given to this book.

For my wife, Gillian

PRO DEO ET PATRIA
In lasting remembrance of those gallant soldier boys
Of Manningtree Road State School
Who nobly responded to their country's call
During the Great War 1914–1919★

From the bronze shield in the assembly hall at Glenferrie School 1508.
The names on the school Honour Board, alas, are missing.

★ The dates 1914–1919 as quoted are correct. Although the Armistice
began on 11 November 1918, the Great War was sometimes
considered not to have officially ended until the Treaty of Versailles
was signed in June 1919.

PRO·DEO·ET·PATRIA

IN LASTING REMEMBRANCE OF
THOSE GALLANT SOLDIER BOYS
OF HARRINGTREE ROAD STATE
SCHOOL WHO NOBLY RESPONDED
TO THEIR COUNTRYS CALL DURING
THE GREAT WAR · 1914 — 1919

AUTHOR'S NOTE

In his short existence of fourteen years and nine months, James Martin didn't leave a lot on the record from which to reconstruct his life story. His six surviving letters home, the letter from Matron Reddock describing his death, and the condolence letter from his mate, Cec Hogan, all generously donated by Jim's family to the Australian War Memorial in Canberra, are reprinted here by permission as an appendix. The letters are published as written, with all that their errors have to tell us about the personalities behind them and the circumstances under which they were composed. I have also included, by permission, an interview with Jim's late sister Annie (Mrs Nan Johnson) and his niece Mrs Billie Carlton, published in the *Sun-Herald* newspaper in 1984; a letter written home by Cec Hogan from Gallipoli; and the 21st Battalion song, which gives an authentic flavour of the times.

I have been privileged to obtain further material from Jim's nephew Mr Jack Harris; his niece Mrs Nancy Cameron; his great-nephew Mr Stephen Chaplin; and Mr Cec Hogan, the son of Jim's mate, to all of whom I am profoundly grateful. The Martin and Hogan service papers from the National Archives of Australia, and records from the Registry of Births, Deaths and Marriages in Victoria and New South Wales have also been important sources of information.

In the absence of other written or oral records, however, I have had to make certain assumptions. For instance, I have assumed Jim joined the compulsory school cadets, that he saw the march through Melbourne in September 1914, and that he stayed with his Aunt Mary at Maldon early in 1915 before enlisting. Many conversations and minor incidents are imagined, as, to some extent, is Jim's personal experience in Egypt, on the *Southland* and at Gallipoli. Wherever possible I have based my ideas on family recollections, or on the letters and diaries of those who were there, as noted in the References. These assumptions seem not unreasonable from the material we have, but further research may throw more light on Jim Martin – the youngest known of all the Anzacs.

Anthony Hill
Canberra, 2001

Contents

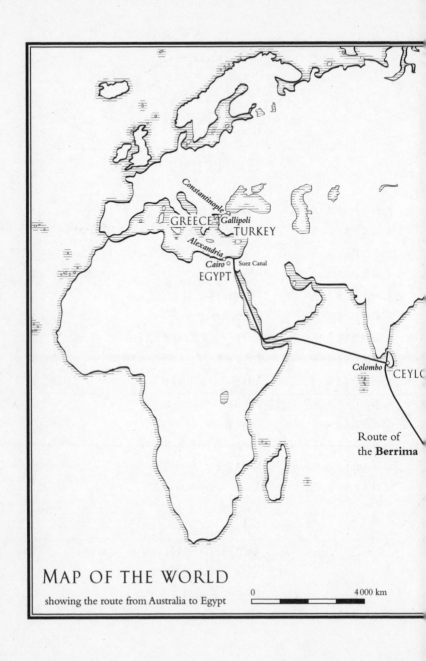

Constantinople

GREECE *Gallipoli*

TURKEY

Alexandria

Cairo ○ ○ Suez Canal

EGYPT

Colombo CEYLO

Route of
the **Berrima**

MAP OF THE WORLD

showing the route from Australia to Egypt

0   4 000 km

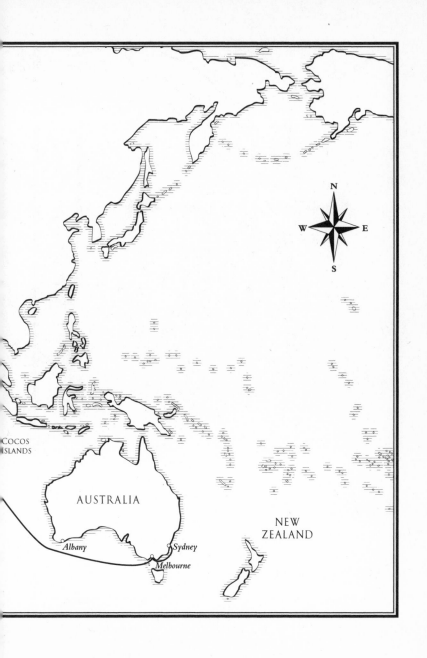

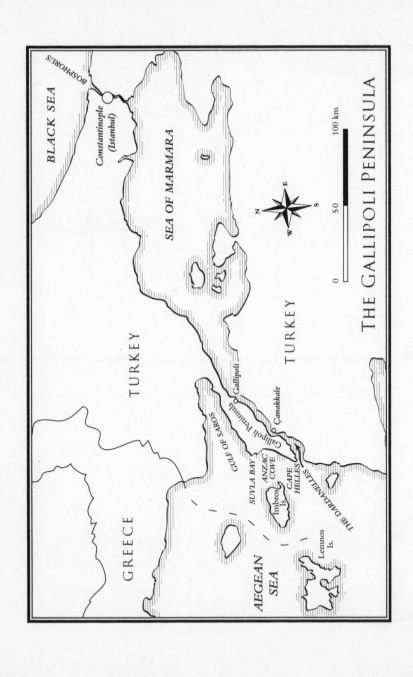

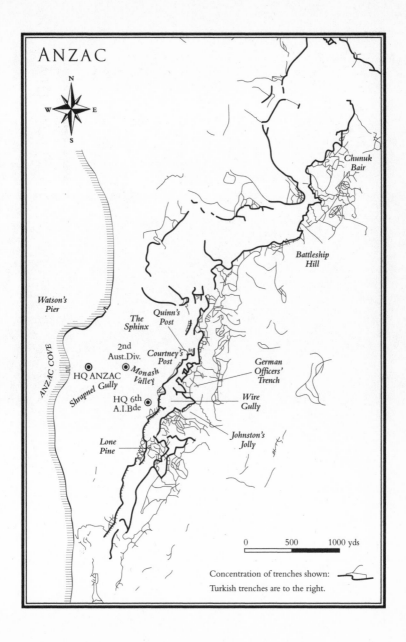

ANZAC

N
W · E
S

Watson's Pier

Chunuk Bair

Battleship Hill

The Sphinx

Quinn's Post

ANZAC COVE

2nd Aust.Div.

Courtney's Post

HQ ANZAC

Monash Valley

Shrapnel Gully

German Officers' Trench

HQ 6th A.I.Bde

Wire Gully

Johnston's Jolly

Lone Pine

0   500   1000 yds

Concentration of trenches shown:

Turkish trenches are to the right.

1: THE *GLENART CASTLE*

In the late afternoon of 25 October 1915, a young Australian soldier – Private James Martin, aged only eighteen so his papers said – lay desperately ill with typhoid aboard a hospital ship, anchored off Anzac Cove, Gallipoli. He was wracked with fever, and his thirst was terrible.

'Water . . .' Jim Martin pleaded through swollen lips. 'Please . . . more water . . .'

But his voice was as weak as he was, and at first nobody heard him. The nurses on board the *Glenart Castle* had done what they could for him – had washed and soothed him – and were busy now with other patients in the crowded ward.

'Please . . . Mum . . . water . . .'

And still they didn't hear.

Jim Martin lay there, exhausted. He could feel the ship rocking beneath him on the swell, so different after those seven weeks burrowed in the trenches on the ridge above Wire Gully. It was warm here, wrapped in a blanket, after the bitter cold and wet of the past few days. Dry. And safe. And someone, like his mother, to look after him. If only they would bring more water . . .

Jim Martin drifted in and out of consciousness on the afternoon tide.

He had been brought aboard the *Glenart Castle* in a state of utter collapse just over an hour ago, in the five o'clock cargo of sick and wounded soldiers who were towed out in barges from Anzac. More sick than wounded. In late autumn, before the weather had turned at Gallipoli, flies and disease were deadlier than Turkish bullets.

So the orderlies carried young Jim Martin on a stretcher down to the ward below decks, and laid him on a bed. His first bed for months. They stripped his uniform, filthy with lice and his own excreta. They cleaned his pitifully thin body: for the young soldier, once tall and strong, had lost half his weight. They gave him water. Such sweet, cool water! In the trenches it always tasted of kerosene.

A nurse gave Jim a shot of morphine, to ease the pain and to help him sleep.

'You'll be all right, soldier. Get some rest . . . I'll be back soon.'

And certainly, as he lay there, Jim Martin began to feel a sense of calm. The burning in his gut and bowels was not so bad, and the vomiting had stopped. The light here was softer than the glare outside, watching from the firing line for any sign of attack from the Turks. It was hot and noisy in the ward, but a fan creaked overhead and air stirred on his face.

'Water . . .'

Jim Martin was wide awake. His throat was as parched as the stony slopes of Wire Gully.

'Please . . . more water.'

Matron Reddock was in charge of the ward that afternoon. She was passing Jim Martin's bed when she heard his cry. So she stopped and bent over the young soldier, her white veil framing her face as he opened his eyes.

'Can I help you, my boy?'

'Water . . .'

There was a glass on the fold-out table attached to the high side of the bed. Frances Reddock put her left arm around Jim's shoulders and, lifting him up, held the glass to his lips. He coughed and retched, but at least a little water trickled down his throat to quench his thirst. For the time being.

Matron Reddock eased his head back onto the pillow. She felt his pulse. It was very 'thready': weak but fast. Too fast. Jim lay looking up at her, as she sponged his sweating brow and spoke softly to him.

'Is there anything I can do for you, son?'

Her English voice, coming from afar, reminded him a little of his mother, Amelia. Jim and his five sisters had all been taught to speak properly, for they came from good family in the past.

'Please . . . am I going to get well?'

'Of course, my boy . . . of course you are.' In her fourteen years as a nurse, Matron Reddock had been trained to give words of comfort and hope to her patients. 'We'll have you up and about in no time.'

Jim Martin smiled back at her. That was good. He'd been afraid. To get sick like that, so soon after he'd told them at home how splendidly he was doing and not to worry about him.

'Thank you, sister,' he said. 'I feel better already.'

Matron Reddock smoothed the dark brown hair clinging to his forehead. She looked at the watch pinned to her lapel. Time was getting on. It was half past six already, and there was much to be done for the other men.

'Try to get some sleep, my boy. It's the best thing.'

As she left him, Private Martin settled down to sleep, rocked in the cradle of the sea a mile off Anzac shore, with drowsy images of youth flitting through his mind.

But suddenly, and quite unexpectedly, Jim Martin died.

A nurse, coming to check his condition, saw what had happened and called Matron Reddock. She felt for the pulse of the young soldier, to whom she'd been talking not ten minutes before. His pulse was no longer there.

'Get doctor! Quick!'

But it was too late. In his collapsed state, infection coursing through his body, Jim had simply let go. He was beyond shock. Beyond pain. His blood pressure falling and heart beating ever more weakly, his system failed. A mere hour and forty minutes after reaching the *Glenart Castle*, Private James Charles Martin was dead. And he was only eighteen, so his papers said.

The army recorded his passing in stark medical language on the casualty form used for soldiers on active service. *Died of syncope after enteritis*. It was the term they used then for typhoid.

Matron Reddock put it more gently, when she sat down the next day, to write to Jim's mother at home with his father and sisters – and a boarding house full of paying guests – at Mary Street, in the Melbourne suburb of Hawthorn.

'. . . he said he was feeling much more comfortable and thanked me *so* nicely for what had been done for him,' she wrote. 'He then settled down to get a sleep but died quite suddenly and quietly of heart failure at 6.40 p.m. That was yesterday . . .'

Frances Reddock paused in her letter and searched for the right words. She had been on the *Glenart Castle* for two months now, but found these letters of consolation no easier to write.

'I know what a terrible grief it is to you to lose him, but you must I am sure feel very proud of him for so nobly coming forward to fight for his country. Yours in all deep sympathy . . .'

Yet exactly what Amelia Martin felt, when she heard of her son's death, not even Matron Reddock could guess.

For they buried Jim Martin at sea the day after he died. His body was wrapped in a canvas shroud, weighted at the feet, and covered with a Union Jack. Reverend Barker conducted the service. Some crew and nurses were there, and a few soldiers not so badly wounded they couldn't pay their last respects to one of their own.

For as much as it hath pleased Almighty God of His great mercy to take unto Himself the soul of our dear brother here departed, we therefore commit his body to the deep . . .

The body slipped from beneath the flag and over the ship's side, to sink beneath the waves.

Afterwards, Matron Reddock made up a parcel of the 'little treasures' that were found in Jim's pockets.

In time they were sent home to Amelia Martin with his other personal effects by the military authorities of the Australian Imperial Force. The aluminium 'dog tag' identity disc from around his neck. A New Testament. Some letters. His money belt. And a thin red-and-white paper streamer: Jim's last link with home as his troopship sailed from Port Melbourne a few months before.

But there was nothing among his papers to show that Jim Martin wasn't eighteen at all.

Nothing to show he'd lied about his age when he enlisted – and that his mother consented to it, because Jim threatened to run away and join up under another name if she didn't.

Nothing to show that, when he died, Private James Martin was in fact only fourteen years and nine months old.

And nothing to say that, so far as is known, he was the youngest of all the Anzacs to die. The youngest Australian soldier boy to sacrifice everything for his country.

2: TOCUMWAL

The military letter confirming Jim Martin's death reached his family three weeks later. It was just at the time of his sister Annie's tenth birthday. Jim had wished her happy returns in his last message from Anzac, and ever afterwards Annie wept when she remembered the grief of that day.

Their mother's hair turned white overnight, from the shock. She was only thirty-eight.

Amelia Martin was a tall, commanding woman, physically strong, and with much strength of character and personality inherited from her own mother. Whatever her despair when Jim died – however much she may have seemed to age – Amelia could not give way to it. For she, by and large, kept the family together.

The three youngest girls – Mary, Annie and young Amelia –

were still at home. The two eldest were married. Esther had already given her a grand-daughter, little Essie; and Alice was expecting in a month or so. Besides, there was the business to manage.

Amelia had long wanted to run a boarding house, just as her mother, Frances, had done in Tocumwal, years ago. It was Amelia who organised the move to the big house, called Forres, in Mary Street, when the lease became vacant. It was she who made it pay. Her husband, Charlie Martin, was a taxi driver and not really interested in boarders. It was Amelia who looked after the guests: going to the early morning markets; organising the kitchen, for she was an excellent cook; supervising the housework and garden, with her children's help.

'I hope your house is full up with boarders and the fowls laying,' Jim had written from Gallipoli, in a letter Amelia received not long before the news that he'd died. And then Jim added that he still hadn't received any of the letters they'd been sending him from home. 'Write soon,' Jim scrawled at the top of the page, 'as every letter is welcome here.'

Amelia's heart broke anew whenever she thought of it. Yet she couldn't give in, at least not during daylight. It was at night, lying in bed, that the tears flowed and she was filled with a sense of self-reproach that never quite left her.

If only . . . if only she had not given in when Jim pleaded to be allowed to enlist and join the great adventure of the War. If only Charlie had been accepted when he'd tried to join up. But he'd been rejected and young Jim said, 'Never mind, Dad, I'll go instead.' She could hear him now. His voice already broken, the boy so manly in appearance, though he'd just turned fourteen.

If only Amelia and Charlie had been firmer when they'd said 'No.' But there was no escaping Jim's threat. 'If you let me go, I'll write to you and stay in touch. But if you don't, I'll join up under another name and you won't hear from me at all!'

'You're just a boy! They'll find out and send you home.'

In the end Jim wore them down. Amelia signed her consent before her husband, and gave her own name as next of kin. Yet the military authorities didn't find out Jim's true age, nor did they send him home. If only Amelia had said something! But what could a mother do? The boy would still make good his threat to run away, and she'd not hear from him again. He could be as single-minded as she was. Now it was too late. They'd never hear from Jim again, anyway. And he'd not received one of their letters from home . . .

At such times, Amelia ached with blame and grief. Though when the tears dried, other thoughts stirred in her memory.

She could see Jim going off to school in his last year, such a lanky boy they'd already bought him his first pair of long trousers. The excitement when he turned twelve and could join the junior military cadets! She remembered him as a youngster, not long after the family moved to Melbourne from the country. And, in the nature of things, Amelia's mind took her back to the busy town of Tocumwal, just across the River Murray in New South Wales, where her son was born and spent the first years of his life . . .

Jim Martin entered the world on 3 January 1901, only three days after people celebrated the birth of the new Commonwealth of Australia.

The people of Tocumwal were all for Federation. There were dances and speeches. People drank the health of old Queen Victoria (though she died that same month). They toasted the local boys who were away with the Light Horse in South Africa, fighting the Boers.

Lying in bed at home, awaiting the birth of her own new child, Amelia Martin could hear the river boats still tooting their Federation whistles down at the wharf.

Mrs Moorfield was the midwife. Amelia always remembered the relief when she heard her baby cry with life, and the joy when she held him to her breast for the first time.

'That's a fine, healthy boy you have, Mrs Martin.'

It was a joyful time all round, with Amelia's family there: her mother, Frances, and her sister, Mary – the children's Aunt Mary – looking after the two little daughters. Charlie came in from work at the general store. He beamed with pride when they showed him his newborn son, and the family drank several bottles of good hop beer to 'wet the baby's head'. They called him James, after Amelia's brother, and Charles, after the father himself.

Charlie Martin was not a Tocumwal man. He'd been born in Auckland, New Zealand. Nor, as they found out much later, was his real name Martin. His father was Samuel Marks, a fruiterer by trade; but Charlie changed his surname to Martin when he came to Australia as a young man, after his parents died. It was easier to do so. There was much prejudice against Jewish people in those days, and names were often changed. So Charlie Marks became Charlie Martin, odd-jobbing his way around before ending up in Tocumwal, as a grocer and handyman at the stores and livery stables. Amelia laughed when she remembered the handsome fellow who swept her off her feet. They married in August 1895, a month before her eighteenth birthday.

Well, life could be short. Amelia's mother, Frances, was only fifteen when she married Thomas Park, a well-to-do young carpenter. They migrated from England during the gold rushes of the 1850s. In the boom years a good builder was in demand. Frances and Thomas travelled the colonies, producing twelve children – Amelia was the youngest, born at Bendigo. Two boys and five girls survived, some of whom settled with their own families in the Riverina district of New South Wales. After Thomas died when Amelia was still a girl, Frances wanted to be close to them. She moved to the town of Deniliquin with her younger children – Amelia, James and Mary.

It was there that Mary met and later married Arthur Pigot, a pub-keeper's son, working as a rabbiter at Howlong Station. Even then, the rabbit plague was destroying much good grazing land. It was also in Deniliquin that Frances, still a handsome, spirited woman at the age of fifty-five, married in 1891 for a second time. Her new husband was George Smith, himself a widower. Not long afterwards, with young Amelia, they moved down the track to the river port of Tocumwal, where Frances opened a boarding house in Murray Street. George took on duties as the cook with Amelia as his teenage apprentice.

Trade was brisk. Frances kept a good table, with meals available at all hours for one shilling, and Tocumwal was a bustling town. When the water was high, paddle-steamers were always pulling into the wharf to pick up and off-load cargoes, wool bales and wheat bags, towed in barges up and down river to Echuca. An astute businesswoman, Frances well knew that Tocumwal was an important border crossing and customs town on the road north from Shepparton. People, livestock and vehicles had to be ferried across the Murray on a punt. Even when the new bridge opened in 1895, the railway didn't cross the river. So there was a constant traffic through town of mail coaches and haulage wagons as passengers and freight travelled between the railheads at Strathmerton and Finley. There was always a call for chaff and hay at the stores where suave Charlie Martin, newly arrived in Tocumwal, served behind the counter and helped the grooms. He'd already caught the eye of young Amelia Park. They began 'walking out' together, as people said in those days. When Amelia was still seventeen (though she said she was twenty-one) and by licence from the Bishop, they wed.

The young-marrieds stayed on at Tocumwal. Amelia already had family there. Her sister Mary and Arthur Pigot moved to town, where Arthur worked as a teamster with the draught horses and heavy drays. Mary and Arthur had two boys by then, Archie and Frank. It was good for the children to be near their grandmother – and also their cousins, as Charlie and Amelia Martin's own children began to arrive.

Esther was the firstborn in July, 1896. Alice followed two years later. Jim, of course, opened his infant eyes in the first exciting days of Federation in 1901, though whenever Amelia remembered that time her happiness was marred by grief. For her own mother, Frances, died in June. She was buried by the Reverend Joseph Ward who, only a month later, baptised the baby James Charles Martin, at the new red brick Anglican Church of St Alban.

For a while, Charlie and Amelia wondered if they should move from Tocumwal to improve their prospects elsewhere. But they stayed. Charlie had work and the tips were good. There were ties of family with Mary and Arthur Pigot and the boys, and they spent much time together.

There was fishing for cod and redfin in the river, and swimming from the sandy beaches on this stretch of the Murray; picnics among the tall river red gums, young Jim with his face full of cream cake; walks through the bush, though they were always on the look-out for tiger snakes; games to play along the low levee banks, built to hold back the water when the river flooded. Even so, Tocumwal was still sometimes isolated by floods that stretched for miles.

There was the life of the town: dances and socials in Hillson's Hall, cricket matches and bike races on Saturdays, the annual district show. Celebrations when the new King Edward was crowned in 1902, and Welcome Home to the boys from the Boer War that same year. Sometimes the cousins sat wide-eyed with delight when a circus visited town, laughing at the clowns and monkeys, and hardly daring to look at the flyers on the high trapeze.

Esther started going to school, trudging with her satchel to Mr Richards, the headmaster, at the schoolhouse. Alice went with her after another year or two, but Jim was still a toddler. He was no longer the baby of the family, though. In 1903, Amelia had her fourth child, Mary. Two years later, Annie was born. Soon after, the family left Tocumwal for Melbourne.

They'd been thinking about it. Now they made up their minds. Mary and Arthur Pigot were going to Germanton, near Albury, where Arthur's dad was taking over the Riverina Hotel. In time they'd run it themselves. Family ties with Tocumwal were loosening. Amelia always retained an affection for the place, but the bright lights and opportunities of Marvellous Melbourne beckoned.

In 1906, Charlie and Amelia, with their five children, caught the coach from Tocumwal across the river to Strathmerton. From there, they boarded the steam train which took them to the city and the rest of their lives.

3: GLENFERRIE SCHOOL

The first years in Melbourne were hard ones for the Martin family. They knew few people in the city, and missed the close circle of friends and relatives in Tocumwal.

Money was tight. Charlie got a job driving a horse-drawn cab for one of the livery stables. He enjoyed it, especially the independence of the road. But his family were growing, and the fares and tips he earned didn't stay long in his pocket. He had to buy boots and clothes and enough food for seven hungry mouths – which eventually became eight. Two years after they moved to Melbourne, Amelia had her sixth and last child, young Amelia, called Millie, named after herself.

It was difficult to find somewhere decent to live. They couldn't afford anything grand, but with six children and two adults the small cottages they rented seemed to burst with people. Amelia was always looking for something better and they were constantly on the move around the inner suburbs. So many moves that one morning, as he left for work, Charlie asked, 'Same address tonight, Amelia?' He could still make her laugh.

It was time to settle somewhere. In 1910 the family moved across the Yarra River to the suburb of Hawthorn. It was a more prosperous part of town. Charlie learned to drive a taxi, for horses then were giving way to motor cars, and the people of Hawthorn could afford his fares. The brick house Charlie rented in Vicars Street was larger, close to the shops and school. That year, at the age of nine, Jim Martin and the older girls enrolled at the Manningtree Road State School.

In her waking dreams, Amelia could still see the children leaving home in the morning, running out the door so as not to miss the nine o'clock bell. The girls in their dark woollen dresses and white aprons, hair tied back with ribbons. Jim in his cap and coat, serge pants down to his knees, long socks and black boots. Slates and books in leather schoolbags slung over their shoulders . . .

There were the children hurrying the half mile or so down Glenferrie Road to school: past Fred Davies's fruit shop and the delicious smells from Melville's, the pastry cook. Past butcher shops and grocers, bootmakers, barbers and Ernest Hill, the estate agent. Through the railway gates and across the road. Past the church and Sam Lee's laundry, stopping outside Elsum's sweet shop to drool at jars of bullseyes and chocolate drops. Then on again quickly as the school bell rang, to line up just in time with the others in the asphalt yard. To salute the flag and recite the pledge: 'I love God and my country; I honour the flag; I will serve the King, and cheerfully obey my parents, teachers and the laws.'

There was a new King in 1910, George the Fifth, whom everybody loved. But it was hard to say that bit about teachers. Discipline was strict. Some teachers were very free with canes and straps – and not just when their pupils misbehaved or made a noise in class, but also for getting their sums or spelling lessons wrong.

Well, there were large classes! With more than 800 pupils, from beginners to grade eight, the school was very crowded. Things eased when they built new rooms and an assembly hall for the younger classes. But the older children still sat at long desks raised in tiers, with the teachers keeping a watchful eye from the blackboard out front. Even then there was mischief. Sometimes the girls' long hair was dipped into the inkwell of the desk behind. And more than once Jim came home bearing the bruises of a fight when someone teased his younger sisters, Mary and Annie.

'You want to make something of it? I'll meet you in the paddock after school.'

The other children would stand round them in a ring, egging the fighters on.

Jim was no angel. He was broken hearted one day. Schoolmaster Hyland made the boys empty all the pea-shooters from their schoolbags onto the ground.

'He stamped on them, Mum! Smashed every one!'

There was a bit of cricket in the schoolyard at lunchtime or a football to kick around in winter, but no organised sport. The children played marbles and jack-bones, at which the girls were good; and the boys often had cockfights, mounted on each other's back. And every day, after recess, the children formed into lines and marched into class to the sound of a drum and whistle.

Jim Martin dearly wanted to play the school drum. But that was a privilege reserved for the older boys who belonged to the school cadet band. In Jim's mind, one ambition merged with the other. He could hardly wait until he turned twelve, and was able to join the junior cadets and play the drum.

At the time, it was compulsory for all boys of this age to begin military training. The famous commander from the Boer War, Lord Kitchener, visited Australia. He recommended an army of 80,000 men, mainly reservists, to defend the young nation and play its part in the wider defence of the British Empire. From 1911, boys aged between twelve and fourteen had to join the junior cadets, training at school. At fourteen, when most began work, they became senior cadets, training at night and in annual camps. At eighteen they enrolled as adults in the Citizen Military Forces.

It was a proud time, a patriotic time in the young Commonwealth. The older boys at Manningtree Road State School were soon formed into a cadet corps. They didn't wear a uniform, much to their disgust – not like senior cadets who wore the khaki battledress of real Australian soldiers. In other respects, though, their training followed correct military lines.

Old Mr Grigg was one of the teachers in charge of them. Every morning for at least a quarter of an hour, the cadets had to do physical exercises – stretching, jumping, running on the spot – strengthening young muscles to make the boys into fit and useful citizens.

'One two . . . one two . . . higher there, young Martin! Put some effort into it!' Mr Grigg shouting through his white moustaches.

They learned the elements of parade-ground drill.

ATTEN – SHUN!

STAND HAT EASE!

How to dress in line . . .

EYES RIGHT!

(shuffle shuffle shuffle)

. . . until the ragged ranks were more or less in straight lines.

They were taught how to march at regulation 120 paces a minute, round and round the asphalt schoolyard . . .

QUICK MARCH!

'Step out briskly, boys . . . shoulders back . . . arms swinging smartly . . . no whistling at the back there!'

SLOW MARCH!

Which was a lot harder. No wonder the cadet drums were needed to keep them in step.

Occasionally the boys even had real rifles to carry. The school built a miniature rifle range, about fifty yards long, against the side fence. From time to time a sergeant or lieutenant from the local regiment would come to school and instruct the cadets in target shooting. They used .22 calibre rifles generally, lighter in weight than the standard .303s. People often used them for rabbiting, and .22s were good for teaching accurate marksmanship. Fairly safe, too, although a red flag was hoisted at the range whenever the boys were practising.

The army was thorough. No boy was allowed to fire his rifle until he learned how to look after it properly. How to oil and clean it. How to load and unload the weapon safely. How to use the sights correctly when aiming, and to rest the butt against his shoulder to take the recoil when it fired.

'Don't PULL the trigger, lad! Squeeze it gently with the ball of your finger!' The sergeant drilling the boys down at the range. Lying beside them on the mat as, one at a time, they aimed at the bullseye.

'Just before you fire, hold your breath to help keep the rifle absolutely still.'

Jim Martin loved it. In time he became a good shot, kneeling or standing, at a stationary or moving target. The boys made their mistakes, of course. Forgetting to keep the rifle pointing towards the target as they were unloading.

'It's for safety, young feller. Make it a habit . . . a instinct!'

One kid was bawled out because he forgot altogether to put on the safety catch and remove his last bullet from the breech.

'You fool! You ass! You could kill yourself or someone else if the rifle went off accidentally!'

And a couple of boys were downright stupid. They didn't want to be in the junior cadets, and more than once pocketed the live .22 ammunition after parade. They removed the bullets, and when old Mr Grigg was out of the classroom tossed the cartridges into the open fire – where they exploded with real risk of injury. The girls screamed. The headmaster, Mr Hamilton, came running. And the room was filled with the stinking smoke of gunpowder. Nobody ever owned up, of course, and the whole class had to write out 500 lines: *I must be honourable and tell the truth at all times.*

One kid practised using three pens strapped together.

On the whole, though, the cadets brought credit to themselves and their school. Most of them, like young Jim Martin, looked forward to the time when they could join the senior cadets. There was public pride in what they were doing.

One day, when she was cleaning up Jim's room after he died, Amelia found a copy of *The School Paper* he'd kept from February, 1913. It had a photo on the cover and a description of a march through the city by over 17,000 senior cadets: the first such parade 'since the law was passed that each healthy Australian boy should be trained to defend his country.'

It took them more than an hour to march past the Governor-General, taking the salute on the steps of Parliament House. True, *The School Paper* said the lads shouldn't be confused with fighting troops. They were only soldiers in the making. Still, 'if so much military knowledge and steadiness can be instilled into boys within a year, the fighting force of 1919, when the scheme will have been fully developed, should indeed be a worthy one.'

If only they knew of the Great War that was coming. If only

they knew how many of those boys would be dead by 1919.

But it was no wonder, Amelia Martin told herself in her grief, that her son should want to enlist, though he was only fourteen. The idea of the boy soldier was all around him. It was there in the junior and senior cadets. Boys could join the new Royal Australian Navy at fourteen to train as sailors, stokers or signallers, and a year younger as cadet-midshipmen. There were songs about brave little drummer boys marching troops into battle during the wars that won the British Empire.

Every year on Empire Day, 24 May, (old Queen Victoria's birthday), there was a bonfire and crackers down at the Glenferrie oval. At school, Headmaster Hamilton – 'Cock-eye' they called him because of his glass eye – would talk at assembly about its glories . . .

'The greatest Empire the world has ever seen! An Empire covering a quarter of the globe . . . all those countries coloured red on the map: Britain, Australia, Canada, New Zealand, South Africa, India . . . An Empire on which the sun never sets, bringing peace and progress to more than 400 million people . . .

'That's why we have to remain strong and vigilant against those nations building arms that might be used against us. That's why the Royal Navy must keep command of the seas! Why we must support the Army and our own schoolboy cadets – our soldiers of the future!'

After which Jim Martin and the band beat their drums. The whole school saluted the new Australian flag, with its Southern Cross and Union Jack in the corner. And they gave three cheers for King George and Queen Mary who reigned over this vast and peaceful Empire.

But neither Headmaster Hamilton nor any of those who heard him – not the chiefs of the army nor even King George in his palace in London, could know how soon or how severely that Empire and the young men who defended it would be put to the test.

4: WAR

So began the fateful year of 1914.

In January, Jim Martin had his thirteenth birthday and started his last year at school. Grade eight with Mr Hyland: a tall, strict man, but a good teacher who was fond of quoting proverbs to show the virtue of hard work.

'Tis better to wear out shoes than sheets.

The pupils in Mr Hyland's class were never idle.

There was English and history, arithmetic and geography. There was Sloyd woodwork class once a week for the boys, and needlework for the girls. There was the cadet corps and the drums to play: for Jim Martin *did* learn the drums, and every morning marched the children into class.

Sometimes, when his sisters, Mary and Annie, were running late, Jim kept on drumming to give them time to rush through the school gate and join the last line. He was a strong, lithe boy, nearly five feet four inches tall and still growing. And he was a good eater. Jim's sisters used to laugh at how much he ate for dinner. But his mother said, 'Leave him alone, it's going into a good skin.'

And there he was, already into long pants for his last year at school, with his tousled brown hair and grey eyes; the drum around his waist and the sticks flying . . .

Mary and Annie were often late for school these days. Mother needed their help at home. For 1914 was the year the lease fell vacant on a boarding house called Forres, just up the hill at 43 Mary Street. Amelia Martin, remembering the place her mother ran at Tocumwal, decided to take it on.

'It's a fine chance to better ourselves,' she said to Charlie. 'There are always people wanting rooms in these parts. The house is almost full with boarders and the rents are good.'

'It'll be a grind,' her husband replied. 'I won't be able to give much help. Not with the taxi . . .'

'I'll manage it myself. It's something I've always wanted to do.'

So Amelia organised the family's removal to Forres: a grand, two-storey house, then about twenty-five years old, built in dark brick, with a bay window in the front and windows opening onto the wooden verandahs upstairs. There were fourteen main rooms, with plenty of ground outside for vegetable gardens, fruit trees and a chook pen: very different from the working cottages the family was used to.

It was still a squeeze, though. Seventeen boarders lived at

Forres together with the eight Martins – less one, when their eldest daughter, Esther, married young Charlie Anderson early in 1914 and they set up a home of their own. Even so, managing the house was constant hard work.

There was wood to be cut for the kitchen range; hot water carried in kettles for baths and washing up; the laundry copper set to boil on wash days, sheets and clothes to be scrubbed and rinsed and hung out to dry in the garden. There was food to be prepared; apples cored and potatoes peeled; dinners cooked; tables set in the dining-room and cleaned away; floors to be swept and beds made. No wonder Mary and Annie were often late for school, and Jim stayed beating his drum for them to hurry up.

Alice had finished school and worked at home. But the younger children were still expected to help – and the boarding house prospered. Amelia was good at it, like her mother. It was in the family blood.

Amelia's sister, Mary – the children's Aunt Mary, whom they knew at Tocumwal – was in much the same business. For some years she and her husband, Arthur Pigot, managed the busy Riverina Hotel at Germanton. When Arthur died, Mary ran the hotel herself until she remarried and sold the pub. By 1914, Mary and her new husband, Bill Musgrave, had moved to the old gold-mining town of Maldon, in central Victoria, where they took over another hotel, the Criterion. Maldon was much closer to Melbourne. Mary often wrote, asking the Martin family to come and stay. Jim was anxious to go.

'I can look for work on the farms,' he said. 'It's the life I love.'

'We'll see,' said his mother. 'You finish your schooling first.'

They had a new headmaster at Manningtree Road in 1914: James McLaren, who was also a Lieutenant Colonel in the reserve forces. He encouraged the school cadets, and talked to them about the growing tensions between the Great Powers of Britain and Germany, Russia, France, Austria and Turkey.

'That's why your junior military training is so important,' he told the boys. 'We may hope international disputes will be settled peacefully. But every country must be prepared to defend itself until the world finds a way of preventing wars between nations.'

At school assembly on Empire Day that year, Mr McLaren again warned of the dangers facing the motherland of Britain and the dominions of the greatest empire the world had known.

'Think what it would mean if our Empire broke up and its members were free to war among themselves, like the nations of Europe who spend a quarter of a million pounds every year on their armies and navies. Think how much less would be our power to keep peace in the world!'

Most of the children – and even other teachers – listening to Mr McLaren didn't take too much notice. They'd heard it before. People had been talking for years of the threats to the Empire and the dangerous military alliances among the Great Powers. But statesmen always resolved every crisis peacefully. Australia had the cadet training scheme, and the country was acquiring a new navy of six major warships and two submarines.

Besides, there were more important things to think about. In the Martin household, for instance, Esther announced that she and Charlie Anderson were expecting a baby in September. There was much excitement. Amelia would be a grandmother for the first time. And young Jim would become an uncle!

So nobody took much interest at the news in late June that the Austrian crown prince and his wife had been shot at a place they'd never heard of – Sarajevo – in Serbia. There was some diplomatic excitement but the crisis, as usual, disappeared.

When suddenly, at the end of July, from out of nowhere it seemed, the world was confronted with war. One by one, the Great Powers mobilised against each other. Austria declared war on Serbia 'to teach it a lesson'. Russia moved against Austria. Germany declared war on Russia and Russia's ally, France. The alliances were dragging them all in.

The question was: would Britain – and Australia as part of the Empire – also be involved in the conflict? Crowds of people gathered outside newspaper offices to read the latest reports. On 4 August, Germany invaded Belgium to attack France. On that day, Britain declared war on Germany. And in Australia, the Prime Minister immediately placed the navy under the overall command of the British Admiralty, and announced an expeditionary force of 20,000 men to be sent overseas within six weeks.

Six weeks!

From all over the country, men rushed to join the newly created Australian Imperial Force: the twelve infantry battalions of the 1st Division, a brigade of Light Horse, artillery, signallers and engineers. They were men who were responding to the call of Empire – to the pledge that Australia would 'fight to the last man and the last shilling': men who were afraid it would be over by Christmas, and they'd miss the adventure.

Wiser heads knew better. With all the industrial might of modern warfare, this promised to be the bloodiest conflict ever.

After a terrible battle near Mons, the German armies advanced quickly towards Paris. But they were turned by the Allied forces. Now, in September, the opposing armies were digging themselves into trenchlines that stretched across northern France at places that were to become household names: the River Somme, Amiens, Peronne, St Quentin . . .

At Manningtree Road, Mr McLaren began wearing his officer's uniform to school. He was often absent on army business leaving Jim's teacher, Mr Hyland, in charge. McLaren was helping to plan the transport of the Australian forces overseas – especially the four Victorian battalions in training at the Broadmeadows military camp. He knew this wouldn't be an easy war, quickly over.

Still, people followed events with great patriotic interest. Everyday occasions seemed less important. Even at Mary Street, the birth of Esther's first baby in mid-September – a little girl they called Essie – passed without the excitement there would otherwise have been. At least among the menfolk. The copies of *The School Paper* and the newspaper clippings Amelia found in Jim's bedside drawer after he died were full of the latest war news and pictures. Jim and his father talked of little else . . .

Of the great battles in France and Eastern Europe. The

despatch of an Australian force to New Guinea in the troopship *Berrima*, and the surrender of the German colony after only a few days' fighting. The loss of Australia's first submarine, the AE1, with all hands, in calm seas off Rabaul. Of the march through the streets of Melbourne by 5000 troops on 25 September, before they embarked for the war . . .

Jim wagged school that day, to see the march with Charlie. He didn't think Mr McLaren would mind – not this once – even if someone else had to beat the drum. It was a dull, damp Friday, with father and son standing among the crowds in Spring Street to see the Governor-General take the salute at Parliament House.

'You should have seen it, Mum!' The boy's voice was breaking with emotion as they sat around the kitchen table afterwards. 'The whole street just lit up! Everybody cheering . . . waving their flags as the Light Horsemen rode by . . . the bands playing when the troops marched past . . . bayonets fixed, eyes right, and everyone in step . . .'

Next morning the *Argus* newspaper said, 'The parade of twelve months ago showed the soldier in the making. Yesterday the Governor-General saw the finished article.' And there indeed was Sir Ronald Munro-Ferguson, saying how Australian troops appeared to great advantage and inspired every confidence.

'I'm thinking of joining up myself,' said Charlie.

'Don't be silly,' Amelia told her husband. 'You're too old at forty-two.'

'I can put my age down to thirty-eight. Lots of men are.'

'You've got a family to support, even with me running the

boarding house. We don't want you getting killed . . .'

The irony of it! thought Amelia, looking at the scraps of news-paper in Jim's room. Yet she could understand the sense of adventure. Even the girls were swept up in it. Annie and Mary were doing odd jobs to raise pennies for the school's Patriotic Fund. They were knitting socks and collecting comforts – tobacco and chocolate – for the Australian soldiers when at last the men left for overseas.

Their departure was delayed for some weeks, much to the troops' impatience. They were anxious to be away, but German warships were raiding ports in the western Pacific. Not until mid-October was it considered safe for the transports carrying the men, horses and equipment of the first contingent, commanded by General Bridges, to sail from Sydney and Melbourne to rendezvous at King George's Sound, near Albany in Western Australia. There they were joined by ships carrying the 8000 New Zealand forces. On 1 November 1914, with a naval escort that included the Australian cruisers *Melbourne* and *Sydney*, the fleet of thirty-eight ships left for the battlefront in Europe.

For the Martin family, as for Australians at home everywhere, news of the sailing did not come until some time later. And there was such a buzz around the breakfast tables when it was learned that, a few days after leaving port, *HMAS Sydney* had found and destroyed the German raider *Emden* near the Cocos Islands. Many of the *Sydney*'s crew were Australian – some of them still boys. It just showed what Australians in action could do! Shells from the *Sydney* set the *Emden* ablaze and, with half his crew killed or wounded, the captain had run his ship aground on a coral reef. *Sydney* picked up the survivors and took them as prisoners to Colombo, where she joined the rest of the troopships for recoaling.

When the voyage resumed, the fleet didn't go to England as expected. Instead, the troops disembarked at Alexandria to spend the northern winter training in Egypt. It would be warmer for them. And now that Turkey had entered the war on the side of the Central Powers – Germany and Austria – the Australians might be needed elsewhere. By mid-December the 1st Division was camped in the desert only a few miles from Cairo. Close by were the Great Pyramids, staring down at humanity as they had for thousands of years.

'I wish I was with them,' said young Jim Martin that Christmas.

'Don't be silly,' said his mother. 'You're far too young.'

'I could put my age up to eighteen. Lots of fellers are.'

'You're not even fourteen yet!' said Amelia.

Little knowing that within a year Jim *would* be with them, and indeed already numbered among their glorious dead.

That December, in its last edition for the year, *The School Paper* printed the words of Rudyard Kipling's poem 'Recessional', which before long would be engraved on stone memorials and on human hearts throughout the British Empire.

Lord God of Hosts, be with us yet,
Lest we forget – lest we forget!

Wounded soldiers being loaded from a barge onto a hospital ship,
anchored off Anzac Cove. [AWM A02740]

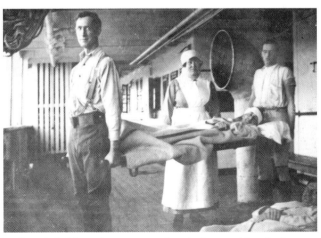

Inside a hospital ship – the nurses and orderlies could only do so much.
[AWM H15309]

Jim Martin's surviving possessions: the table centrepiece, the paper streamer, his dog tag and money belt, Memorial Plaque and Scroll.

[Courtesy AWM]

Jim's maternal grand-mother Frances Smith

[Courtesy members of Jim Martin's family – Jack Harris, Nancy Cameron, Stephen Chaplin]

A store at Tocumwal, where Jim's father Charlie Martin worked behind the counter and helped the grooms c.1895.

[Courtesy Elaine Bate and Lynne George]

Troops marching along Spring Street, Melbourne – confidence, patriotism and pride. 25 September 1914 [AWM J00352]

Forres, the boarding house in Mary Street, Hawthorn. 'A fine chance to better ourselves.' [Courtesy Margaret Francis]

Jim with his five sisters, 1915. From left to right: Annie, Alice, Millie, Esther and Mary. [Courtesy members of Jim Martin's family]

'Never mind, Dad. I'll go instead.' The recruiting office, Melbourne Town Hall, during the First World War. [AWM J00320]

5: JOINING UP

Christmas came and went. They didn't celebrate it with the same gusto as usual. The war was on and people expected to make sacrifices. But after New Year and Jim's fourteenth birthday (which Amelia did celebrate as always with an iced cake and candles), Jim went to visit Aunt Mary and Bill Musgrave at Maldon, where he planned to find work.

There was plenty in the bush for a strong, healthy young lad to do. Farmers were short-handed. So many country boys rushed off to join up when war was declared that there were not enough hands to bring in the crops.

So, during the long, hot days of January and February, Jim worked with the teams of horses and harvesters in the paddocks. By night he sat with his aunt and uncle at the Criterion Hotel, sipping beer and listening to the talk in the bar: of the weather;

the latest war news; what was happening in Europe; what was likely to happen with the men of the 1st Division of the AIF still training in Egypt. It was the life Jim Martin always thought he wanted . . . a world of men, of hard work in the out-of-doors, and the slow, ever-changing pace of the seasons.

And yet . . . it wasn't enough for him. Not now. Not when the second Australian contingent was already arriving in Egypt. Not when news came through in late February that the Allied fleet had started bombarding Turkish forts guarding the Dardanelles, that narrow strip of water between the Aegean Sea and the Black Sea. They were trying to force a passage through the minefields and capture the city of Constantinople. But the Turks were bitterly opposing them, and in a great battle on 18 March they had sunk several British and French warships.

As summer at Maldon turned to autumn when these events were happening on the other side of the world, farm work was not enough for Jim Martin. Not when new Australian infantry brigades were being raised, with the 21st, 22nd, 23rd and 24th Battalions at Broadmeadows camp forming the 6th Brigade. And especially not when a letter arrived from home saying that Charlie had tried to enlist. But had been rejected.

'Never mind, Dad. I'll go instead!'

So Jim said to himself.

Saying little to Aunt Mary, he caught the Melbourne train one day in early April, to tell the family what he intended to do.

'You can't!' his mother cried. 'You're too young . . . you're only a boy . . . tell him Charlie!'

'It's a brave thing, Jimmy lad,' said his father. 'A decent thing, to want to join. But you don't *have* to do this . . .'

'I've made up my mind, Dad. If they don't want you, they can have me instead.'

'But you're only just fourteen!' His mother was weeping.

'I can pass for eighteen, Mum.'

Indeed Jim Martin could. His skin had tanned and toughened over these past few months in the open. His muscles were strong. He weighed nine and a half stone, and stood five feet six inches tall. Jim's voice had broken and puberty had passed early. His body hair was growing and his genitals had developed all the characteristics of a sexually mature man. Oh yes. Jim Martin could pass for eighteen.

'But you mustn't go to war! You don't realise! Let others risk their lives!'

'And have me miss all the fun?'

'You're still a child, Jim! They'll find out and send you home!'

'Who'll tell them, Mum? You?'

'We won't give our consent, will we Charlie? You know every soldier under twenty-one has to have his parents' agreement to go overseas. We'll refuse.'

'You wouldn't!'

'Yes, we would.'

The atmosphere was electric. Two stubborn minds, mother and son, each wanting to dominate the other. Charlie between them, trying to be the peacemaker, and the younger girls crying.

'Jimmy, boy . . . you've got to see reason . . .'

'I've decided, Dad. The choice is up to you and Mum.'

'What do you mean, son?'

'If you let me go – if you sign the consent – I'll write to you and stay in touch. But if you don't . . . well, I'll run away and join up under another name, and you won't hear from me at all.'

His potent threat.

'You'd not do that, Jim?' His mother's voice was cracking. 'You can't do that to us!'

'I can. And I will, if you don't sign. I wouldn't be the first.'

'No!'

For days the argument raged through the boarding house. Up and down stairs. At the woodheap. In Jim's room. His parents trying to talk the boy out of his folly; the lad just as determined to persist.

'I told you. I've made up my mind.'

'But this is a *war*, son. It's not a game. It's not school cadets. Thousands of men are being killed every week in France. You've seen the papers.'

'I'm no coward, Dad. I'm not afraid.'

'But *I'm* afraid!' cried Amelia. 'What will we do?'

'You know what I'm going to do, Mum. Give your consent, and I'll keep in touch. If you don't, I'll go anyway . . .'

Jim had already started packing his few things. He meant what he said. So that, in the end, Amelia Martin gave way. She sat at the kitchen table and wrote on a piece of paper: 'I hereby consent to my son James Martin joining the Expeditionary Forces.'

She signed and dated it 10 April 1915. Charlie signed after her.

He was more hesitant, wanting to insist that Jim stay home. But Amelia persuaded him.

'He says he'll run away! He says we won't hear from him again. And Charlie, I couldn't bear that . . .'

Thus, at last, Charlie signed his consent too.

Two days later, on a wet Monday morning, amid tears but also a certain pride at his gallantry and patriotism, his family kissed Jim farewell. Waving to some of the boarders who stood on the steps of Forres to wish him good luck, he went out the gate carrying his kit bag. He walked to Glenferrie station and caught the train to the city. And there, Jim made his way up Swanston Street to the Melbourne Town Hall and the recruiting office of the Australian Imperial Force.

In after years, Amelia always remembered Jim telling her that the enlistment officer had said Jim was the fittest specimen he'd seen that day: standing in line with fifty or so other men who had volunteered; filling in his papers at a long wooden table; Jim giving his age as eighteen, a farm labourer by trade, his parents' consent attached. It was considered sufficient proof of age. No birth certificate was required. Tellingly, though, Jim gave Amelia as his next of kin. Charlie's name was written in much later.

Then to the medical room, every inch of Jim Martin inspected for signs of disease or a defect which might make him unsuitable as a soldier. Sight, hearing and intelligence good. He hopped across the floor on one foot and back again with the other. His teeth were sound, and he could say 'Who comes here?' in a loud voice, as required. There were no head lice. Height, weight and chest measurement were all within regulation. They'd recently lowered the minimum height – though one man went to pieces when told that, at five feet three and a half inches, he was still too short.

'I've given up me job and everything,' he cried, 'and I'm knocked back for want of half an inch! It's not fair.'

The army could afford to be choosy. More men were coming forward than were needed. But in time, when recruiting became harder as the casualty figures rolled in, the height was lowered to five feet two inches and even five feet, as the maximum age was put up from thirty-eight to forty-five.

'The fittest specimen we've seen all day,' said the attesting officer, Lieutenant Dalton, when Jim presented him with the

Medical Officer's certificate. And then, holding the Bible in his right hand, Jim took the Oath to well and truly serve the King until the end of the War; to resist His Majesty's enemies; and in all matters of service to faithfully discharge his duty according to law.

'So Help me God.'

'Welcome to the army, soldier.'

His pay was five shillings a day. Six shillings when he embarked for overseas and became, as the soldiers joked, one of the 'six-bob-a-day tourists' – though one shilling was deferred pay until service was ended by death or discharge.

That afternoon, in the first good rains of the year, the new recruits went by train to the Depot at Broadmeadows. They brought their razors and soap with them, an extra suit, a change of underclothes, a second pair of boots and a coat.

Over the next few days they were given their basic uniforms from the quartermaster's store. Khaki service jacket, not too tight, with deep pockets at the chest and waist, and khaki cord breeches. The felt slouch hat, left side turned up, so distinctive and so loved by every Australian soldier, though for a time they also wore the small, peaked British service caps. Grey flannel shirt and woollen underclothes. Tan ankle boots and – hated by almost every-one – strips of cloth called 'puttees', wound around the leg from ankle to knee for some support and protection. Off duty around the camp, the men wore blue dungaree overalls and soft, floppy white hats against the sun and rain.

Some things were late being issued, however: their heavy

woollen greatcoats and waterproof groundsheets. There were many complaints about that at the time Jim went into camp. As the April rain poured down, Broadmeadows became sodden. Without groundsheets, the straw-filled mattresses on which the men slept eight or ten to a tent got damp; and without greatcoats, their clothes were always wet. Amelia Martin wasn't the only one who worried about the risk of pneumonia among the troops.

Families came out at weekends, squelching through mud, to see the Light Horsemen on parade and to watch the great horse-drawn guns of the artillery on manoeuvre. But mostly they came to see how their menfolk were coping with the routines of army life . . .

Reveille at 0615 hours and wash in canvas buckets before parade at 0700. An hour of physical exercise and drill. Breakfast at 0800, the men from each tent moving in lines past the cook-house, a tin plate for stew and bread in one hand and a pannikin for coffee in the other. More drill at 0900, marching round the parade ground by section, platoon and company. Rifle drill. Practice and instruction with full-sized .303s at the range. Dinner at 1300 – meat, bread and potatoes – and either a route march with full pack or more drill in the afternoon. Skirmishing. Learning to move quickly and surely under fire to attack an objective. To obey every order by instinct. Being taught how to use the bayonet.

PARRY! THRUST! ON GUARD!

And there were always officers to salute and call 'sir'. There were always the non-commissioned officers, the NCOs –

sergeants and corporals and lance-corporals – whose every word was law and who must never be answered back, even when they were wrong.

Discipline. Discipline. Discipline.

Amelia thought Jim would soon get sick of it and want to come home. That he'd own up he was only fourteen and get discharged.

But he didn't. Jim loved every moment of the life. No, it wasn't playing, like school cadets. It was real life. A soldier's life. Even the hardships and monotony of more stew and tea at 1800, one tin of jam for each tent, with milk and butter to be bought extra from the canteen – these things were real.

As was the companionship of the men with whom he shared that life. Older men like Alf Leonard, who was thirty-eight and a railway porter living with his wife in the hills – until he joined up the same day Jim did, and was to go on to win the Distinguished Conduct Medal. Some, like Arthur Lee, were still in their teens – though none were as young as Jim Martin, even if he never let on.

He watched them and copied them: adopting the swagger and rougher language of older men, pretending to an experience he did not have. He would go with them at night to the tent fixed up as a stadium to watch boxing matches – grudge matches, often, between soldiers – and concerts. Sometimes, before the bugle call to retire and Last Post at 2130, Jim went to the Salvation Army tent which had a piano and books, pen and ink. And, as promised, he wrote home.

'Dear Mum and Dad, just a few lines hoping all is well as it leaves me at present . . .' His letters always started the same way. It helped get some of those awkward words on the page. He went on to tell them about some missing pictures. 'I seen about those photos this evening. He had sent them to the wrong Martin . . .'

A few days earlier Jim had been granted leave, and went into town to have his photograph taken with his sisters. There they are, fixed for ever on the print. Jim so tall and casual in uniform between the five young women. Esther and Alice sitting in cane chairs, looking pensive. Mary, Annie and Amelia standing almost to attention in their dark dresses, white collars and bows in their hair. They took a number of poses. A close-up of Jim in his peaked cap. Another standing next to young Millie, perched on top of a plant stand. And who, unless they were told otherwise, could say that Jim Martin did not look eighteen?

Afterwards, they went back to Mary Street for tea. Cakes and biscuits fresh from the oven, much better than the slabs of bread and rationed jam at Broadmeadows. The whole family was there. Esther's daughter, little Essie, and Charlie Anderson who was talking of joining up too. But Jim told him not to be silly!

'You're a husband and a father now,' he said. 'There are plenty of single blokes like me who should go first.'

'That's right,' said Esther.

Alice was seeing a young fellow called Percy Chaplin. He was a military policeman, stationed at the South Melbourne barracks. Percy was also at tea and he greatly admired Jim's spirit.

'Good on you, lad.'

But when he found out Jim's true age, he was sworn to secrecy. The whole family was afraid Percy Chaplin would consider it his duty to report the fact to the military authorities. And what then? Not only had Jim lied about his age, Amelia and Charlie Martin had gone along with it. Was that perjury? Could they be punished?

How often, in time to come, did Amelia wish she'd not made Percy Chaplin keep his silence? If only he *had* said something to someone higher up in the military . . .

Yet Jim's threat was always there, hanging over her like a doom. *If you let me go I'll write to you and stay in touch. But if you don't . . .*

Besides, it was too late. Jim was committed. The whole country was committed. Just two weeks after Jim Martin enlisted, Australian and New Zealand troops went into action. With British and French forces, they invaded Turkey: landing at a place on the Dardanelles coast few had then heard of, but which was to echo around the nation.

Gallipoli.

6: LEAVING

The landings on the Gallipoli peninsula took place at dawn on 25 April 1915.

After the Allied fleet failed to force a passage through the minefields guarding the Dardanelles, a land invasion was planned to silence the Turkish forts and clear the way to Constantinople. The Turkish Army, with their German advisers, used the time well to strengthen their positions on the rugged Gallipoli peninsula. When the Allies attacked, the defenders were waiting for them.

The main body of British forces landed at Cape Helles, at the foot of the peninsula. The Australian and New Zealand troops came ashore at a sandy cove to the north, below a range of three steep ridges leading to the summit of a hill the Turks called *Koja Chemen Tepe*, the Hill of the Great Pasture, which dominated this part of the battlefield.

They landed at first light on Sunday morning. Silently, under cover of darkness, the first assault troops filed from the transports anchored offshore and into strings of row boats which were towed by steam launches to the beach. At the tillers sat young naval midshipmen: mere boys, it seemed. At 0429 the first shot rang out from the heights above. As day broke, the fire became more and more intense. It seemed to rain bullets and death. Some men died still sitting in the boats. Some were hit and dragged down by their heavy packs while wading ashore. Many were killed racing across the beach to the cliffs. 'The key,' one Anzac said, 'was being turned in the lock of hell.' But still the young midshipmen kept ferrying their boatloads of soldiers to shore – showing a courage the men who survived that day never forgot.

Night currents had carried the boats further north than expected. Instead of flat, open country, troops faced ravines and sharp, scrubby hillsides. Men and companies became separated as soldiers fought their way up to the first ridge . . . to the second ridge . . . A few of them got to the third ridge, for a brief view of the Dardanelles, before Turkish forces led by Major Mustafa Kemal counter-attacked and pushed them back . . . Back to the second ridge and defensive positions about half a mile inland.

By nightfall, 16,000 men had landed. By nightfall, more than 2000 were dead or wounded. By nightfall, General Bridges realised his troops were unlikely to take the third ridge. Through the Anzac commander, General Birdwood, he asked if they shouldn't withdraw. But there wasn't enough time before dawn, nor enough boats. The commander of the Mediterranean Expeditionary Force, General Hamilton, sent back the message, 'There is nothing for it but to dig yourselves right in and stick it out.'

So stick it out, they did. Through eight months of bitter fighting. Dig themselves in, they did. Into trenches and saps, dugouts and snipers' nests, sometimes separated from the Turkish lines by only a few yards. Digging in at places they called Quinn's Post, The Nek, Lonesome Pine . . .

The cove where they landed they named after themselves. Some time after arriving in Egypt their infantry brigades had been formed into a corps, the Australian and New Zealand Army Corps. The initial letters were used as a post mark on mail sent home: ANZAC. As 'Anzacs' they became known. The word gained currency. At Gallipoli it gained meaning. So they called the little beach Anzac Cove.

News of these great events reached people at home four days later. The newspapers were filled with reports of the gallantry and boldness shown at the Gallipoli landings.

Something tremendous had happened! For the first time our soldiers had been tested on the ancient battlefields of Europe, and had not been found wanting. For the first time they fought not as Victorians or Queenslanders – but as Australians. Army recruiting figures doubled and trebled as men rushed to be part of it.

For wives and mothers, of course, the war came ever closer. The first casualty lists appeared in early May. No one was immune. General Bridges was shot by a sniper and died three days later on 18 May. Next day, shrapnel killed a humble stretcher bearer, one Private Simpson, carrying the wounded on his donkey.

For men already encamped and in training, the news from Gallipoli was immediate and intoxicating. They, too, could soon expect to be sent there! Their rifles, aimed at targets down the range, would soon be shooting enemies. The bayonets they stuck into straw dummies would soon be pushed into living flesh.

PARRY! THRUST! TAKE *THAT* YOU FILTHY TURK!

It couldn't come quickly enough.

At Broadmeadows Depot, Private James Martin was assigned to the 1st Reinforcements of the 21st Battalion and given his regimental number – 1553. The battalion had been forming since March, and even now was getting ready to leave for Egypt. Fighting troops constantly needed new men to replace casualties. When the 21st Battalion sailed in the troopship *Ulysses* on 8 May, Jim and the reinforcements still in training knew it wouldn't be long before they joined them.

Besides, in mid-May came more glorious fighting at Gallipoli. The Turkish army launched a massive attack to push the invaders back into the sea. They were met by devastating fire from the Anzac trenches. In a few hours, 3000 Turks lay dead and dying in no-man's-land. It roused the blood lust in those still at home. If only they, too, could have their share of killing!

But then something curious happened. On 24 May – Empire Day – Turks and Anzacs arranged an eight-hour truce to bury their dead, now stinking and rotting under the sun. Soldiers from both sides took advantage of the break in fighting to leave their trenches, to exchange cigarettes and talk in broken bits of language. Before going back to kill each other. Strange. Fraternising with the enemy!

Indeed, something even stranger was happening. Among the Anzac diggers, the mood began to change. Instead of hatred and contempt for their Turkish opponents, a sense of respect developed. Turks, too, were brave in the face of terrible fire. They, too, stuck by their own. They, too, shared the same hardships. The nicknames 'Abdul' and 'Jacko Turk' became terms of – if not friendship – at least of fellow-feeling.

Yet these things the reinforcements at home didn't know. Nor could they, until it was their turn to land on that shore.

Amelia Martin hoped and prayed they wouldn't send her son away just yet. Not when there was still time . . . surely . . . for *someone* to find out he was only fourteen, and send him home for good. Except, she knew, it wouldn't be for good. Jim would find a way to go to this war, whatever they did. So, on his brief visits, she fed him. And kissed him. And when he went back she gave him a photo of herself and Charlie in the back garden of Forres, smiling grimly into the camera. It was one way to remember.

'I'll send you some photos of me and the blokes in our tent,' said Jim.

'I'd rather have you here with me.'

'Come on, Mum! We're expecting to go overseas any time now.'

As it turned out, they went to the army camp at Seymour, north of Melbourne, to complete their training in early June. It was just as the 21st Battalion arrived in Egypt and marched into base at Heliopolis, near Cairo. Seymour was much less exotic. A dreary plain with a few trees and low hills. The same rows of tents and horse lines as Broadmeadows. The same stews. The same drills. The same route marches across country. The same rain pouring down.

'The road up here is no better than Broadmeadows,' Jim wrote home. 'In fact it is a lot worse it is just like soup.'

He asked them to send him more warm underwear, and the girls were knitting khaki socks to help keep his feet dry in the mud and slush. But something went wrong, and the parcel didn't turn up at the railway station.

Few families made the train trip to Seymour at weekends. The place was miserable in the wet. Jim missed them. Besides, the rumours were flying. They were going on Monday! They were sailing on Wednesday! He might not see his people again. So one Saturday after parade, Jim slipped away from camp and caught the train to Melbourne. He was Absent Without Leave – a serious military offence. If caught, Jim could be charged and confined to the guard house. But he didn't care. Time was short. And lots of blokes nicked off briefly. It was worth the risk.

Saturday was always best at Mary Street. It was baking day.

When Jim arrived home unexpectedly, Amelia gave him a huge tea of cakes and scones that she and the girls took fresh from the oven. Alice's boyfriend, Percy Chaplin, wasn't there – luckily. You wouldn't want a military policeman about the place when you were Absent Without Leave!

They sat around the table, telling Jim their news. School had closed for a couple of weeks and was being fumigated because of an outbreak of diphtheria, from which several children had already died. They told of a grand patriotic concert at the Town Hall, and fund-raising for war relief. And they asked him a thousand questions. About Seymour, and was he used to sleeping on a straw mattress yet? Had he got the parcel? And did he like the scarf young Millie was knitting for him?

Afterwards, Jim walked around the garden with his parents, each of them wondering if it might not be for the last time.

'Do you know when you're sailing, son?'

'It can't be long, Dad. We keep hearing different days.'

'You'll let us know, Jim. We want to see you off.'

'Course I will.'

'Jim, it's not too late! You could still change your mind . . . tell them your right age. They won't be too hard on you.'

'Mum! We've been through that! I told you, I can't back out now! Anyway, I've assigned most of my pay to you. They'll send it every fortnight.'

'It's not money I want, Jim! It's *you* I care about!'

'Don't, Mum! You're just upsetting yourself and me, and I don't know when I'll be home again . . .'

So Amelia and Charlie bit their lips and fought back the tears. And when Jim left to get his train back to camp, they kissed and hugged him at the front door. Saying goodbye. And the whole family gave him a brown leather belt to wear under his jacket. It had a little money pouch – and inside, they tucked a five-pound note. Mary, Annie and Millie walked with Jim to the railway station. The same way they always walked to school.

'I caught the 6.35 train from town on Saturday night', Jim wrote in his Monday letter, 'arrived here about 9.30 and they did not know I had been away so I am wright as rain . . .'

Spelling was never his strong point.

They heard that day their departure had been postponed yet again. Jim tried to send a telegram to let his parents know. But the post office wouldn't send cables about troop movements. Security.

On Thursday, though, came the news they'd all been waiting for. Hats were thrown into the air and men crowded into the canteen to celebrate with a glass of whatever they fancied.

'Dear Mum and Dad,' Jim wrote from the Salvation Army recreation tent. 'We are told we are going Monday now for certain. We could not go before until we had completed our shooting. We were down the range on Tuesday and Wednesday shooting, and I passed my Musketry . . .'

It was still raining, Jim told them, but his parcel of underclothes had arrived at last. He enclosed some more photographs, and asked that one be sent to Aunt Mary at Maldon.

It was a photo of himself, standing to attention in his uniform.

His slouch hat, looped up on the left side, the Rising Sun badge of the AIF on his lapel. A soldier boy of only fourteen, looking serious beyond his years. Vulnerable too, of course. But then, so does every soldier about to leave for war.

They spent the next few days packing their equipment. Oiling rifles. Sharpening bayonets. Cleaning boots and webbing till they shone. The sense of excitement was everywhere. Men laughed at the adventure on which they were about to embark. If they also felt apprehensive, well, they tried to keep it to themselves.

Such emotions couldn't be hidden by their families, however. On Saturday, they got twenty-four hours final leave. Jim went home to Melbourne in the crowded train for the last time.

It was a solemn, sombre family who sat down to dinner that night. Esther's husband, Charlie Anderson, tried to keep everybody's spirits up by saying what a grand thing Jim was doing and how he wished it was himself.

'No, you don't,' said Esther.

'You have got everything? Enough warm socks?' Amelia, too, was trying to be bright. Trying not to say what was really on her mind. The time for argument was past.

'Everything, Mum. It's summer over there. We'll be warm enough, I reckon.'

'You *will* be all right . . . ?'

'He'll be fine. It's turning into stalemate on Gallipoli. Neither side can break through.'

Percy Chaplin, the military policeman, knew about these things. He was almost family. Percy and Alice were getting married: in fact, though it was kept very hushed, Alice was already pregnant.

'You mustn't worry about me, Mum,' said Jim.

'I can't help it. I look at the casualty lists in the paper and the pictures of the wounded men in hospital . . .'

Charlie said, 'Then we must try to be as brave as Jim.'

But in the silence of the night, Jim could hear weeping from his parents' room. He pulled the blankets over his head, however, and tried to shut the sound from his ears. He could bear nothing to disturb his own excitement at leaving.

He went back to Seymour next morning. The following day – another wet Monday, 28 June – they broke camp and marched to the station where the train was waiting.

A few hours later, corporals and sergeants shouting orders, they reached Station Pier, Port Melbourne. The troopship *Berrima*, just arrived from Sydney with the 20th Battalion, was already berthed. The band played 'Tipperary' and 'Australia Will Be There', though men scarcely heard it for the beating of their own hearts. They formed into columns and slung their packs. With heads high they marched through the crowd of families and friends, and up the ship's gangway.

Jim found himself a place by the deck rail. He looked for his parents and sisters among the faces below. He couldn't see them at first. And then . . . there they were! Waving and shouting farewell, and blowing him kisses.

Goodbye! Good luck! God be with you, son!

The liner blew its siren and bells rang. Tugboats gathered steam. Gangways were pulled away and the ship's ropes cast clear. Those watching on the wharf threw hundreds of streamers, like a paper rainbow, to the men crowded on board. Cheering. Waving. Sobbing. Jim caught a streamer, red-and-white, and, holding it, leaned over the rail as the ship began to move. He peered through the billowing colours for his family somewhere in the crowd: catching glimpses, in these last few moments, of his own mortality.

'Goodbye Mum!' Jim cried. 'Goodbye Dad! Write to me . . .'

A gap opened between the pier and the ship's side. Wider and wider, as they moved into open water. Smoke poured from the funnel. The propellers sprang into life. The streamers pulled and strained. One by one they snapped and fell away as the *Berrima* moved under her own power.

'Auld Lang Syne' played the band, and 'God Save The King'. Until the notes were borne away on the wind. The faces of those on the wharf grew blurred and distant, and at last disappeared altogether as the troopship steamed down the bay.

They were going! The bit of red-and-white streamer could no longer hold Jim Martin to the land of his birth.

He put it away for safekeeping. And went below.

7: THE *BERRIMA*

Thus Amelia Martin remembered her son as she last saw him: Jim crowded at the ship's rail, cheering and laughing and flushed with adventure; Jim draped in streamers, as the *Berrima* pulled away from the pier.

What happened after that, Amelia knew only from letters and the souvenirs he sent home from Egypt. But she couldn't tell – as mothers *can* – what her soldier boy really felt. She wasn't there when Jim got sick at Gallipoli. She wasn't beside him through that last awful hour on the hospital ship . . .

rocking . . .

sweating . . .

calling for water . . .

Jim felt a cool, wet cloth on his brow . . . an arm around his shoulders, lifting him and holding a glass of water to his lips. He heard a woman's voice, not unlike Mum's, through a misty, white veil as he opened his eyes . . .

'Thank you.'

Jim lay back on the pillow. His body felt as nothing. Empty. Floating. But at least there wasn't the pain any more of last week . . . wracked with vomit and cramps until he couldn't stand up . . . couldn't hold his rifle steady in the trench at Wire Gully . . . couldn't even keep down any water, and his throat on fire . . .

'Please . . . am I going to get well?'

'Of course, my boy.' The voice, like his mother's.

His heart feebly pumped morphine through his veins. After the fears and agonies of the past week, Jim sensed relief. He'd be all right. Right as rain. When he'd told them at home he was doing splendid . . .

He lay there, slipping in and out of wakefulness, aware of the ship's motion. It reminded him of those nights on the *Berrima*, men swinging in their hammocks as the ship steamed across the Indian Ocean. Even better, when they got to the tropics they were allowed to take their bedding on deck. The night air was so cool after the heat below, as they lay watching the stars come out, brighter than Jim had ever seen them. He could hear his mates around him talking, playing cards and having a smoke until Last Post at 2200 and lights out . . .

Fragments of memory fluttered through Jim's mind. Smoke? Course he smoked. They all did. Tried it, anyway, until Jim thought he'd cough his heart up. The other blokes wetting themselves, as he did the drawback and his eyes turned to water.

'Enjoy that, Jim! Make a man of you . . .' his mate, Cec Hogan was laughing. Cec would carry his tobacco pouch, water-stained and tattered, with him right through the war.

There was no smoking between decks, though. Risk of fire, and strictly forbidden. There was a corporal . . . what was his name? . . . who'd been reduced to the ranks when caught. And Harry Johnson was given two days' fatigues. Two days scrubbing decks and paintwork!

They found Jim, once, scratching his name in the paint on the companionway stairs. It was a pretty silly place to break a rule. He was put on mess duties for a week. Peeling spuds. It wasn't so bad, not when the others were all out on deck in the heat doing drill. Or listening to lectures on map reading. Or learning semaphore signals with two coloured flags . . .

Talking to the crew, as he sat peeling his potatoes, Jim learned a lot about the *Berrima*. They were proud of her. She'd already played a gallant part in the war.

'I was with her taking the troops up to Rabaul after the war broke out, and they seized New Guinea from the Germans,' said a mess steward. 'Saw a bit of shooting, too. And last January we towed the submarine AE2 behind us all the way to Suez.'

Australia's second submarine had covered herself in glory. A few days after the Anzac landing, the AE2 found a way through the minefields guarding the Dardanelles and into the Sea of Marmara. But the sub was unlucky. It was damaged by Turkish gunfire, and the crew had to sink the vessel and surrender.

A few months earlier a British submarine, commanded by Lieutenant Norman Holbrook, had braved the same minefields to sink a Turkish battleship. Unlike the AE2, Lieutenant Holbrook's sub returned safely and he was awarded the Victoria Cross. His name became famous. Even as the *Berrima* steamed towards Colombo, the town of Germanton, in southern New South Wales, where Jim Martin's Aunt Mary had once run the Riverina Hotel, was patriotically changing its name to Holbrook.

They held three parades every day on board the *Berrima*. Reveille at 0600, the bugle echoing through the ship. Wash in cold water, roll up your hammock, and half an hour of physical jerks before breakfast. Parade again at 0930 for two hours of drill.

SQUAD – SHOULDER – HARMS!

Sergeant Anderson shouting above the sea sounds.

SQUAD – STAN-DAT – HEEZE!

Boat drill, too, so they'd know what to do if the ship got torpedoed and sank. Useful that, in time to come. How to put on a life jacket. Which lifeboat was yours and how to board it . . .

Dinner, and two hours' parade again, though nothing too strenuous in the heat of the tropics. Sometimes they had rifle shooting from the ship's side, to keep up their skills. Or lessons in first aid: how to dress a wound, and mend a broken limb.

'Hey!' shouted Charlie Nunn, when Jim was trying to strap a

splint. 'If me bloody leg's not broke now it will be when you've finished!'

Poor Charlie would die of wounds in France next year.

They lined up for more inoculations by the medics against enteric fever and just about every other disease they could think of.

'There's not a germ left that could live in my arm,' said Bob Lowry.

Pity, though, for young Jim Martin lying so ill aboard the hospital ship with typhoid, that the vaccine didn't always work . . .

But then, they couldn't help the flies . . . the stinking, filthy flies of Gallipoli, feeding on corpses and living in open cesspits . . . crawling into your mouth as soon as you opened it to eat. Swallowing them, like a plague. No wonder men got sick . . .

Jim's brief connections of thought flickering.

The food on the *Berrima* was always good. Porridge for breakfast. Roast for lunch and heaps of vegetables. Especially potatoes! Milk for your tea and coffee, and plenty of butter. Lots to eat. Except when it got rough. The plates slipped up and down the galley tables, and blokes rushed to the ship's side to heave it all up again. Fred Goodman spent half the voyage leaning over the rail.

Mostly, though, when parade was over, it felt like a holiday for these 'six-bob-a-day tourists'. There were concerts at night, deck quoits and sports days when they all went in for sack races. There was a bit of boxing. And Jim and Cec Hogan sat on a spar bashing away at each other in a pillow fight. Until they fell off together and became best mates.

Sometimes, during those long, lazy afternoons, the two young soldiers would stand on the shady side of the deck, watching a school of dolphins leaping through the ship's wake. Yarning. Talking of home and families. Sharing confidences.

'You heard of Ned Kelly?' Cec asked.

'The bushranger? Hanged in Melbourne? The Kelly Gang . . .?'

'Yeah. My family knew them.'

'Gorn . . .' Jim disbelieving.

'Fair dinkum. We lived next door to the Kelly's in Greta West. Mum knew his sisters and his cousin, Tom Lloyd, who made Ned's armour, and she nursed old Mrs Kelly when she was sick . . .'

'That true?'

'Honest injun!'

'You still live there?'

'Nah. Dad's a builder. We moved to Benalla. I was still going to school when the war . . .'

'School?' Jim exclaimed. 'What d'you mean . . . school?'

'Nothing . . . A mistake . . . I . . .'

Cec Hogan drew a deep breath. How far could he trust this mate?

'You keep a secret?'

'Yeah. Sure. What?'

'I said I was eighteen on the enlistment form. But I'm not

really. Put my age up. Said I was a butcher. But I'm not really. My mate, Bob Briggs, is the butcher. I was still at high school when I told them, "Bob's joining up and I'm going too".'

'What did your people say?'

'They carried on. Dad swearing. Mum crying. The headmaster saying, "You're top of the school and you mustn't leave." But I said, "I'm going anyway, and if you try to stop me I'll run off and join under another name".'

'Me, too.'

'Thought so.'

They slyly looked at each other in the late afternoon light. And laughed. Jim's secret was out.

'How old are you really?' he asked Cec Hogan.

'Sixteen. Seventeen on October 26th. And you, Jim?'

'Same. Sixteen. Same as you.'

Jim looked away, as if the sun burned his eyes. Half his secret was out, at least. He dare not trust himself . . . or trust anybody with the whole truth. Not even a mate. The merest slip, and he could be sent back to Australia and have to start all over again. He knew of quite a few fellers of sixteen or seventeen who'd got away with putting their ages up – but none as young as himself.

'Tell us about you, Jim.'

So he told Cec about Amelia and Mary Street, the farms at Maldon and Charlie's rejection.

Never mind, Dad. I'll go instead.

But he let the lie of his real age sit between them. It was safer that way.

Two weeks out from Melbourne they 'crossed the line' at the equator. One of the crew came over the ship's side dressed as King Neptune. Everyone was shaved with foam and had their heads ducked in a tub of water – officers and all! Talk about fun, when they wrote home.

Best, though, was Colombo, on the island of Ceylon, where the *Berrima* stopped to take on coal. It was the first foreign city most of the men had seen. The ship stood out to harbour, tugs and coal barges coming and going, and natives dressed only in loin cloths swarming on board and jabbering away.

'I dive! I dive!'

They were diving after silver sixpences the soldiers tossed from the top deck, coming up grinning and waving, and clambering back aboard.

'I dive again!'

They were pretty good, and lucky not to break their necks. The water wasn't all that deep!

In the afternoon the troops went for a long march around the city: past the shops and red-roofed mansions of the European quarter, the gardens dripping with bright, perfumed flowers; past the hovels where the natives lived, all trying to sell over-priced fabrics and jewellery and cigars to the passing parade.

'You buy banana? Sweet banana?' Little kids ran after them in the dust.

'How much you want?'

'Sixpence each, sahib.'

'Thief! I'll give you sixpence for the whole bunch.'

'One shilling and sixpence, sahib.'

'One shilling.'

'Very well, sahib. You are a hard man, sahib.'

The blokes dearly wanted to ride in a rickshaw – the little open carts pulled by the native men. But they weren't allowed. So after tea, Jim and Cec Hogan went ashore anyway without permission. 'French leave' they called it. They weren't the only ones. And they went for their rickshaw ride, up into the hills and the tea plantations, giving the runner a whack on the shoulders with a bamboo cane if he didn't go fast enough. It was the custom.

Of course, when they got back to the ship, an officer was waiting to take down names. More punishment fatigues! Jim and Cec Hogan slipped unnoticed through an open porthole.

The *Berrima* left next morning, heading back into the Indian Ocean. Shipboard discipline resumed. But there was still time to watch the flying fish like small aeroplanes skimming the water, to feel the rain on their skin when a storm broke, and to stand by the ship's rail looking at the blue haze of the Arabian coast as it hove into view.

They passed through a Strait they called 'The Gate of Tears' and into the Red Sea, the sunset the colour of blood. These soldiers neared their destination and wondered what might happen . . .

There was Harry Barker, who was to become a sergeant and show great presence under fire in France, winning the Distinguished Conduct Medal; the Francis brothers, Ted and Frank, who also lived in Hawthorn and had enlisted at the same time as Jim Martin. Both were in their twenties. Both were killed on the same day at The Somme in 1916.

Now's the day, and now's the hour;
See the front o' battle lour!

. . . the lines of Robbie Burns, from the little book of verse Cec Hogan also carried with him throughout the war. It was a present from home. He knew the poetry by heart, and would quote it from time to time.

All of them were wondering, but not knowing, as the *Berrima* docked on 26 July at Suez, where they were to disembark, with Sergeant Retchford shouting his orders:

'Hammocks rolled up ready for inspection. Blankets folded square in four folds and placed in piles for checking. Mess tins to be thoroughly cleaned. Any questions? Right then!'

They left the ship for the railway station in marching order, carrying rifles and kit bags, their water-bottles filled. The train journey took six hours. The line ran through desert beside the Suez Canal for some distance, and for the first time these troops really saw the louring 'front o' battle'. The Turks were active in the area, and both banks of the canal were entrenched and patrolled by Allied soldiers.

The railway branched away at Ismailiya. And passing through Zagazig they crossed irrigated country, green with maize and date palms, until they reached the great city of Cairo sprawled beside the River Nile.

8: EGYPT

Like all the Anzacs, Jim Martin and his mates were fascinated by the sights and smells of Egypt.

There were the mosques and minarets, crowded streets and bazaars; hawkers and beggars; women, mysterious behind dark yashmak veils; fat men in suits wearing red fez caps, or flowing past in Arab robes. All the clamour and potent odours of the strange and exotic.

Feluccas sailed the broad waters of the Nile, where peasant *fellahin* cultivated the rich river floodplains in the timeless traditions of the centuries. In the city, opulence and marble and ancient magnificence stood side by side with squalor and poverty and dark, dirty alleys that made the dens of Little Bourke Street in Melbourne look like paradise.

Impatient troops, fresh from the *Berrima*, had to wait to savour

Cairo's delights, however. The train took them to a railway siding near Heliopolis, a fairly new suburb just outside the city. From there, they marched in full uniform carrying their kit, to Aerodrome Camp some miles away.

After a month at sea, it was hard going. The desert, which looked rather picturesque from a train window, was a grim place outside. It was even crueller during the weeks that followed. The new reinforcements faced a tough training schedule to bring them up to the same level of fitness and readiness as the whole battalion.

A few days after the reinforcements arrived at Heliopolis, the platoons of the 21st Battalion had their group photographs taken: men staring formally but gamely into the camera, wearing not only their Anzac uniforms but also the pith helmets that British Tommies always wore in the tropics.

When, in mid-August, the 1st Reinforcements officially joined the battalion, Jim was assigned to 4th Platoon, A Company, under Sergeant Henry Coates. There were four platoons of about forty men in each of the four rifle companies which, together with officers, signallers, pioneers, machine gunners, transport and headquarters staff, gave a battalion strength of over 1000 men.

The platoons were further divided into four sections of ten men under a corporal. Jim and Cec Hogan were together in their section. This was good. They were mates. They shared their secrets. They were part of that close-knit bond of fellowship without which soldiers cannot fight effectively in battle – let alone survive the rigours of training in the Egyptian desert!

There was sand. Sand everywhere. Sand in your mess tin, in your boots, in your blankets, and in your eyes when the wind blew. Sand that harboured gnats and fleas and crawly things when you were out on night attack exercises with sister battalions of the 6th Brigade, or on picket duty back at camp.

Sand and heat. The sun rose like a burning eye as you slogged through an early morning route march, scorching the sand when they had you digging trenches; turning the camp huts into ovens during lectures on manoeuvres or signalling. Heat leapt up at you from the paved streets of Heliopolis – the very name meant 'City of the Sun' – when you strolled into town of an afternoon.

There was that, at least. In the Egyptian summer, troops in training usually had the afternoons off. Reveille might sound ungodly early. But between lunch and parade at 1700, the time was generally your own. To write letters home, or read your mail if there was any. To go into town if you felt like it, to buy postcards or gifts, and to get a snack for only a couple of piastre – a few pence – at the Broadmeadows Cafe. The names were just like home! They even had a Luna Park at Heliopolis – until it was turned into a hospital.

Jim and the others often went in after tea. You had leave, so long as you were back for rollcall at 2200 and lights out. He bought handkerchiefs for Amelia and Charlie, and 'Twenty-four Nice Views of Heliopolis' for his sisters. And one Sunday after Church Parade, when they went into Cairo (only half an hour on the electric tram), Jim stopped at a stall in the bazaar, and ordered his mother an embroidered centrepiece for the table. The souvenir sellers ran it up on a sewing machine from the design Jim picked.

Amelia looked after it well over the years: a square of white cotton, polished like satin, with a silvery blue fringe. Jim chose a red star and crescent moon in each corner, with a date palm, the pyramids, the Nile, and a sphinx (grinning like the Cheshire Cat) in the middle. There were two flags, the Union Jack and the French Tricolour. Above the picture, in purple, were the words, *A souvenir from Egypt. Cairo 1915*. And below, in blue, he had written, *To Mother from Jim. Good Luck*. With violets and daffodils.

The Anzacs sent souvenirs like this home by the thousand. Some would be turned into cushions. Some would be framed and hung on the wall. Some would be carefully put away. But however familiar and worn they became, there would still be something ineffably poignant in the naïve sentiments they conveyed.

Jim left his order. And while his gift was being made up, he went to the pyramids with Cec and his mate, Bob Briggs, the butcher. A whole group of them went. They took the tram across the river, and rode the last bit of the way on donkeys. They climbed up the great pyramid of Cheops, where the first Anzacs had planted an Australian flag and carved their initials into the stones. They saw the real Sphinx, her nose shot away by Napoleon's soldiers, but still staring inscrutably over the desert as she had for 6000 years.

They explored the tomb of Kephron, sliding on their bums down a long, low ramp, and crawling on stomachs through a tunnel into the burial chamber to see the pharaoh's coffin. It was a cold, dank place, carved with hieroglyphs, where an old Egyptian told the soldiers' fortunes by torchlight for half a piastre each.

He rooked them. Their fortunes were all the same! He said they'd all go home heroes. Even Bill Farrell. But like Jim, he'd not leave Gallipoli alive.

While they were there, Cec Hogan jotted down sketches of the pyramids and the camels. He bought a postcard of the designs and hieroglyphs that decorated the temple walls and mummy cases, and copied them out in his notebook.

'You draw pretty good,' said Jim, admiring his work. 'You should be an artist.'

'I want to be an architect,' said Cec, 'if I get home in one piece. I was going to be, too. Doing well at school and then . . . I didn't want to miss this fun.'

Doing well! He was dux of his class. It was why his mother was so upset.

'You've got the chance of a good education, son, and you're throwing it away in the military!'

Emily Hogan had a good education herself. A bush nurse and midwife, and close friend of Ned Kelly's family, she also wrote articles for the *Bulletin* magazine, kept the Benalla Registry of Births and Deaths, and became a Justice of the Peace. It was from her that Cec got his love of poetry and interest in the world around him. The family had little money, but Cec was one of the few working-class lads of his time who went on to high school.

'You've got talent, boy. You could win scholarships. You could become whatever you wish!'

So said his headmaster, pleading with Cec to stay at school and not run off to war. Though when the boy insisted, he said it was 'like finding a pearl in the sand, and seeing the waves wash it away.'

Cec kept that bit to himself. A feller didn't embarrass himself by talking a lot of guff.

Still, there was something about Cec Hogan – something in his ability and manner – that stood out from others. He was a mate worth having. In France, Cec was to become a sergeant: almost the only one of his whole platoon left alive after an attack. But they couldn't know that during their first innocent month in Egypt. Even if they had, it would have made little difference.

One afternoon they visited wounded soldiers, evacuated from Anzac and recovering in the Australian General Hospital at Heliopolis. It was a huge place, converted from a hotel, with thousands of beds filled with sick and injured.

Men blinded by shrapnel pellets and wounded by flying metal. Men with limbs blown off. Men with their flesh burnt and their bodies punctured by bayonets. Men who spoke of new and terrible battles in early August, as the Anzacs fought to break the Gallipoli stalemate and capture the high ground.

They told of three days' bitter fighting with bomb and bayonet, much of it underground, when they captured and held the Turkish trenches at Lonesome Pine: a dreadful fight that entered their collective memories. Lone Pine, as it became known, cost them more than 2000 casualties.

They told of 230 Light Horsemen killed as they charged in waves against Turkish machine guns on a narrow strip of land they called The Nek . . . Of more Anzac assaults up the ridges as the British made another landing at Suvla Bay . . . Brave and glorious, but in the end failing to reach the heights, as both sides fought to exhaustion.

These things the boys, fresh from Australia, heard from the wounded off the hospital ships. But far from making them wish they'd stayed at home, the effect was the opposite.

'I just want to be at Anzac *now* and able to take their place,' said George Broadbent. 'I'm sick of Egypt. I'm sick of training. I want real work to do.'

George was eighteen and, like Jim, came from Hawthorn. He was to get his real work. He won a Military Medal with Percy Mortimer as a runner for Brigade Headquarters under heavy fire in France.

In any case, they hadn't long to wait. Things were stirring. In mid-August the 20th Battalion, with whom they'd sailed in the *Berrima*, was ordered to Gallipoli to take part in a last attempt by the Anzacs to cross the peninsula.

'It's not fair,' said Jack Piggott.

'Why can't it be us?' asked his brother, Frank.

It couldn't be them because the 21st Battalion was otherwise engaged. For eleven days, its men formed part of the Cairo city garrison – the first Australian troops to do so – although the newly arrived reinforcements were kept in training back at camp.

From the beginning, Egyptians had been alarmed by rowdy Anzac behaviour. Mothers warned naughty children the Australians would get them! There'd even been riots in the brothel district known as the 'Wasser', the most recent only a few days after the 1st Reinforcements arrived in camp. Furniture was smashed and a piano thrown out the window. Five houses were torched, and when the fire brigade arrived Australians cut the hoses. Men were protesting at lousy beer, high prices charged by the women, and the way their mates who caught venereal disease were treated by the military. They were confined behind barbed wire in camp, their pay books stamped 'VD', and they were often sent home.

'Disgusting . . . disgraceful . . . men unable to control themselves,' sniffed the officers.

'Don't the silly beggars know that soldiers always face danger on active service? Clap from the harlots and bullets from the enemy,' said older, more experienced diggers.

They saw the battles in the Wasser as a bit of fun, men letting off steam. But the authorities took them seriously. The 21st Battalion's stint with the city garrison was a gesture of peace and goodwill. Yet within days of their return to Heliopolis, rumours swept Aerodrome Camp. They were leaving for Gallipoli!

Rumours became fact. At parade the Commanding Officer, Lieutenant Colonel Hutchinson, announced they were breaking camp next day. Everyone started cheering. The band, practising near by, broke into the ragtime tune 'Sailing Down the

Chesapeake'. Some blokes started dancing the cakewalk and – sensibly – parade was dismissed early.

'Dear Mum and Dad,' wrote Jim, 'We are going tomorrow, Friday 27th August, to the Dardanelles to have our share of the Turks. I hope to be . . .' Jim paused, thought, scratched out the words and wrote instead, 'I think I will be well in it by the time you get this letter. We are packing up now.'

He'd been 'going pretty solid' this past fortnight, he told them, getting fit. He'd not received any mail from home, but perhaps he hadn't been in Egypt long enough to get a return from one of his own letters. His few gifts had been given to a wounded chap returning to Australia, and he asked if the family had got them yet.

'I will try to write as much as I can over there. There is nothing to tell you as everything is Desert and work . . .'

He sent his best love to them all. Aunt Mary and Bill Musgrave, his sisters (with a question mark after Alice, was she married yet?), Mum and Dad. And nine kisses. 'I remain your loving Jim.'

Then he remembered. 'Many happy returns to Mary and Alice and Mum's Birthdays. Be sure to write soon.'

Jim addressed his letter and took it to the mailbag. He needed a good night's sleep. They were striking camp in the morning, for the Dardanelles. He was going to be ready for it.

9 : THE *SOUTHLAND*

Jim Martin woke briefly from his dreams. He felt the water lapping against the hospital ship, riding on the sea swell. White light touched his eyes. He heard voices, drowsy and distant, and drifted into thoughts of another day. Another voyage. Another ship . . .

The *Southland*, out from Alexandria, with a thousand men of the 21st Battalion on board, bound for Lemnos Island and Gallipoli. A troopship full of soldiers, like sitting ducks, about to be torpedoed by a German submarine . . .

Remember that time, getting ready to go! They broke camp with much excitement – and then had to hang around Heliopolis for another two days! Which meant sleeping out and getting wet. The desert may be hot as hell by day, but at night it's cold and the dew heavy.

A big mail arrived on Sunday. Some men got more than twenty letters and newspapers from home. There was nothing for Jim Martin. He turned away and asked himself if they had the right address. Were they even writing? Other reinforcements got mail, so what was wrong . . . ?

Jim tried to push such thoughts aside.

Late that afternoon, well before the bugler sounded Fall In, the men were all on the parade ground, dressed and standing easy. Then to Attention! And with the band playing 'Liberty Bell', they marched to the railway siding and the train that was to take them to the port of Alexandria. More waiting. They didn't leave until dark, and arrived at the wharf fairly rowdy at 0230. Blokes who managed to sleep on the train floor were roused, shouted at, formed up and, with daylight breaking, marched aboard the transport *Southland*.

She was a fine-looking liner with twin funnels, at one time part of the German passenger fleet and known as the *Vaterland* – the Fatherland. But she'd been seized by the British when war broke out, and given a new name and occupation, carrying troops.

Or trying to. Once again, the battalion and others sharing the voyage to Gallipoli – some signallers, an artillery brigade, B Company of the 23rd Battalion – spent the day waiting on board. They were anxious to be on their way, but were delayed by the big brass who were to join them: Major General Legge who commanded the 2nd Australian Division, with his headquarters and signal staff, and the headquarters of 6th Brigade – their own brigade – under Colonel Linton.

The battalions who landed at Anzac and had already won such renown were the 1st Division of the AIF. The 2nd Division, to support and relieve them, had been formed in July from three new brigades: the 5th Brigade (17th to 20th Battalions from New South Wales), the 6th Brigade (21st to 24th Battalions from Victoria), and the 7th Brigade (25th to 28th Battalions from Queensland, South Australia and Western Australia).

Each battalion had its own spirit and self-identity, to which men held with a fierceness of pride and loyalty that lasted down the years. From the beginning it was there in the 21st Battalion to a high degree. That afternoon, as the *Southland* waited at Alexandria and the band gave a concert, men broke into the battalion song they'd first sung on the voyage from Australia.

Here's luck to the old Twenty-first
Here's luck to the bold Twenty-first,
For the flag of our country will float higher
When held by the proud Twenty-first.

The words had since been drilled into the new reinforcements. But none of them knew how much luck they were going to need.

The *Southland* finally left Alexandria late on 30 August, with the transport *Haverford* carrying the 23rd Battalion. Men quickly settled again to the routine of shipboard life: sleeping in hammocks on the troop decks; morning and afternoon parades. They were given life jackets and shown their boat stations, though the chances of their being needed seemed remote. Britannia and the Royal Navy ruled the waves. Few thought about enemy submarines lurking *beneath* the Mediterranean. There was no anti-submarine drill on board and the *Southland*, under Captain Kelk, was only lightly armed as it steamed for Lemnos Island, where the whole brigade was assembling for the final voyage to Anzac itself.

The excitement and tension rose higher the closer they got. They were almost there! They were going to have their share of action and glory. If there was any doubt at what fate might decide, men hid it under wisecracks. They were mostly young, and all were invincible. Death, on a battlefield, comes for somebody else.

It was a short trip of only three days. On the last morning, 2 September, Jim Martin came on deck early to join the troops already waiting and eager for parade at 1000. They were only a couple of hours out from Mudros Bay.

Jim and his mate, Cec Hogan, stood by the *Southland*'s starboard rail, looking through the clear, blue morning at an island passing in the distance.

'It's Strati, I think,' said Cec. 'Not far to go now.'

Behind them, they were aware of men talking to their mates; having a smoke; checking their gear. When suddenly there was a cry. Some of them on the port side saw the dark conning tower of a German submarine break the surface. They watched, horrified, as the sub fired – and the wake of a torpedo sped towards the ship.

'Oh, Christ! We're gunna be hit!'

For all of them time seemed to hang, suspended, waiting for the inevitable.

Moments later the *Southland* shuddered with the impact. There was a massive explosion forward of the bridge. A gaping hole opened in the hull, and a smaller one opposite as steel stanchions supporting the troop deck were blown out the other side, killing several men. A huge waterspout rose into the air. Captain Langley, all polished up for parade, was blown sky high and flung through a forward hatch into the bilges. Seawater poured in. The ship began to list and her bows sank into the waves.

Bells rang and whistles blew.

Men rushed shouting onto the deck. 'What's happening? Have we hit a mine? Was it a torpedo?'

At the stern, the gunner opened fire. The submarine fired again, but too late. The second torpedo missed the ship's stern by a few yards. Those watching saw the sub dive beneath the surface and disappear.

On deck, there was initial confusion and uncertainty. Men were running everywhere. But when the siren blew to abandon ship, the troops knew exactly what to do. Jim and Cec and the others without their life jackets went below to get them. They returned quickly and stood with their platoons at their allocated lifeboat stations, almost as if they were doing a drill. There was a sense of discipline – even calm – that would remain long in the memories of those who survived.

But panic broke out among certain of the *Southland* crew,

especially the stokers. In his dreams, Jim Martin could see them still . . . tumbling onto the deck, yelling their heads off.

We're hit! We're sinking! We'll all be drowned!

Some of them rushed the lifeboats, jerking and tugging at the cables, leaping in to save themselves without a thought for the soldiers waiting by the rails.

'Come back or I'll fire!'

Captain Kelk appeared from the bridge, holding his revolver. Two of the crew had successfully launched a boat, and were rowing away.

'I order you! Pull back!'

Captain Kelk fired a warning shot above their heads – and then another.

'Aye . . . sir . . .'

Reluctantly the boat returned to the ship's side and took off a group of waiting soldiers.

Others weren't so fortunate. Some lifeboats stuck to the paint-work and had to be prised away, such was their state of wartime readiness. Some cables jammed in the davits when they lowered the boats. Men had to lean out over the ship's side to free them. But all at once the cables would run loose and the boats plunge to the water, overturning and spilling their occupants into the sea.

Many drowned that way. There were two boys . . . Jim could see them still behind his closed eyes . . . two cabin boys, no more than twelve years old, who climbed out on the davits to free a boat. The ship suddenly lurched and heeled further to port. The boys were flung overboard screaming, and were dragged under the waves.

The *Southland* settled deeper into the water. It seemed as if she were about to sink. But the engineers shut the bulkheads soon after the torpedo struck and surprisingly, despite the heavy list, she stayed afloat. There were a number of rafts and collapsible canvas boats on the rear deck. Some of the soldiers and remaining crew worked feverishly to get them launched. One by one, as their names were called, men moved forward and took their places. The boats were launched and they pulled away from the ship's side.

The troops' behaviour was remarkable. It was only four months since the liner, *Lusitania*, had been sunk by a German submarine with the loss of 1200 lives. And everybody remembered the sinking of *Titanic* in 1912. So far as they knew, the men on the *Southland* would soon join them. But still they patiently waited in turn for their allotted boats.

'What was the name of that island?' muttered Jim. 'I'm scared stiff I'll never see land again.'

'Me too, mate,' replied Cec Hogan under his breath.

But who would be the first to admit it out loud, or betray that sense of collective steadiness?

A few, in the platoons behind Jim, played cards. Captain Langley, who'd been blown into the bilges, returned exhausted to his place on deck. Somebody started to sing 'Australia Will Be There'. Somebody else called out 'Are we afraid to die?' and they all bellowed in reply, 'NO!'

The beginnings of a soldier's life – Broadmeadows Depot – routines, drills, peeling spuds, and the companionship of men. [AWM P0858/08]

Charlie and Amelia in the garden at Forres, 1915

[Courtesy members of Jim Martin's family]

Anzac Cove – crowded with troops and supplies. [AWM P02226.022]

The Australian General Hospital at Heliopolis. 'It was a huge place . . . thousands of beds filled with sick and injured.' [AWM H16957]

Men on the *Southland* after it was torpedoed, preparing to abandon
ship. [Courtesy Elaine Bate and Lynne George]

Rescued men from the *Southland*. Several naval vessels, and the hospital
ship *Neuralia* seen here, picked up survivors. [AWM H12827]

Jim's mate,
Cec Hogan, 1915.
Still a schoolboy
too, but two years
older than Jim.

The 21st Battalion climbing to the ridge. Up and up. It was hard
enough going without carrying the extra weight of full packs.
Gallipoli, 8 September 1915 [AWM A00742]

'Are we downhearted?'

'NO!'

There were even a few jokes.

'I can't swim, Sarge,' said one bloke to his NCO. 'But this is the best bloody chance I ever had of learning.'

By 1015 – half an hour after the torpedo struck – two thirds of those on board had got away. The problem was with the boats on the starboard side of the ship. They were hard to launch because of the list, and the soldiers were inexperienced in handling them.

'Next!'

Men of the 4th Platoon of A Company, Privates Martin and Hogan among them, moved forward and took their places in the boat.

'Lower away.'

The boat swung out. It jerked and shuddered, dropping down on the stiff cables. It banged heavily against the side of the listing ship. Someone leaned over to try to push the boat away, and was lucky not to be crushed.

Bit by bit they descended towards the water. Over halfway there! When suddenly the cable holding the stern of the lifeboat jammed. But the fall at the prow, taking up the slack, ran loose. The boat pitched forward. And the men were hurtled into the sea.

Down. Down. Down.

Jim felt the water closing about him, cold and all-consuming. Dragging him down to the darkness in his shirt and breeches.

He'd taken off his tunic and slung his boots around his neck. But they were gone, and even now were following him to the bottom.

Deeper and deeper. Until his breath could hold no longer. Frantically, Jim began to push with his arms and legs. Pushing upwards through the water to reverse the fall . . . upwards through the streaming bubbles to the light and air of the surface . . .

He broke through and gasped. Jim filled his lungs with oxygen, but got a mouthful of seawater as well. Coughing. Half choking. Sinking briefly beneath the water again, but supported by the cork blocks in his life jacket.

Jim thrashed his arms and for a moment began to panic. He saw other men floundering in the water. He called and tried to reach them, but he was carried away by the fast-flowing current. Panic rose in him again and he shouted.

'Help! Help me!'

Still was he swept further away from the others, until he seemed to be alone in the wide, glittering sea. He struggled and cried. But finding that the cork supported him and that his head stayed above water, Jim's inner voice told him, 'Keep calm.' To save his strength, if he was to have any chance.

He took a deep breath. Then another. And slowly began to dog-paddle. Nothing too hard or tiring, but enough to keep him moving. His limbs seemed to be working. No bones were broken that he could feel, except his ribs ached where he'd struck the side of the boat in the tumble. Thank God the sea was smooth, though the current was sweeping him rapidly away.

Wreckage floated near by. Oars and a life belt. A corpse – one of the stewards in his white jacket, the blood seeping from a head wound – lolled helplessly past. The first dead body Jim had seen.

'Jesus!'

Part of an up-ended boat came towards him. Jim struck out and clung tight as it bobbed and eddied in the water.

He looked around. He was a long way from the *Southland* where men, like ants, were clearing the last of the rafts. On the horizon, Jim saw the first faint plumes of smoke from the ships that had picked up the radio SOS and were steaming to the rescue.

Jim still couldn't see any of his own companions. He waved and yelled again.

'Cec . . . ! Sergeant Coates . . . !'

But he heard only the sound of his own voice and the wind whipping across the surface. Were they drowned already?

Jim called again. For anyone.

Nothing.

He drifted in the vast emptiness. He was alone. Even the sense of time passing seemed to have abandoned him.

'Help me!'

Jim heard a voice calling faintly across the water. Straining his eyes in the silver glare, he saw – or thought he saw – an arm waving from a figure some way off.

'Help me!'

'Hang on, mate! I'm coming!'

He began to paddle and kick, trying to swim on the upturned wreck to the drowning man. But the swell came up, and the current ran, and the more Jim tried the further away he was carried.

'Help me!'

Until the cries faded on the wind.

Jim Martin clung on for his own life. The sun beat down. On and on he went, heaving with the sea and feeling the cold seep into the marrow of his bones. He was afraid he'd pass out, that he'd slip off the wreckage and become one of the drowned himself. Salt cracked his mouth, and his throat was raw with thirst . . .

'Help me!'

Sobs were gathering in his guts.

'Help me . . .'

'Hold on there, old chap!'

A voice sounded close by. Hands reached out to grab him.

Jim turned. A lifeboat full of men was beside him, easing their oars. The hands seized him and helped him to the side of the boat.

'Easy there . . . Can you lift yourself up?'

Jim used the last of his strength to scramble aboard.

'No, no. We've got too many already. He'll tip the boat . . .'

He opened his eyes and saw an older man – one of the crew, a stoker by the look of him – shouting from the stern.

'Throw him back . . .'

'Shut up, you!' came several voices in reply. 'Any more lip like that, and we'll throw *you* back instead.'

The man was silent.

'You okay?' asked the man in charge, a corporal from one of the other companies.

Jim nodded. He coughed and spewed seawater. A couple of blokes from his own platoon had also been dragged aboard. He saw Cec Hogan over there . . .

'I'm a bit buggered though,' Jim said.

And he fainted face up in the bilge water.

10: MUDROS BAY

Jim didn't know how long he lay there. It might have been minutes. It seemed like hours. When he opened his eyes every bone in his body ached and his mind was numb with shock. He lay very still, watching the clouds roll across the sky, as the lifeboat rose and fell on the Aegean Sea.

He was roused by his mate's voice.

'Feeling better?'

Cec had swapped places with a bloke on the seat near Jim.

Private Martin grunted.

'I'll live.'

'Good-oh.'

They said nothing further for the moment. They didn't need to. Their gratitude that the other was safe lay in the intimacy of silence between friends. Until it was broken by the voices of men talking excitedly.

'Look Corp! Look over there! The old *Southland* ain't done for yet. She's getting up a head of steam!'

Jim raised himself on an elbow.

'Wakey, wakey, sunshine,' said the corporal. 'Welcome back!'

The others laughed.

Cec helped Jim haul himself onto the seat. He looked out to sea. Black smoke was rising from the funnels of the *Southland*. She was a long way off but the ship, imperceptibly, seemed to be moving.

'She's still afloat,' he croaked. 'She's under way again.'

Indeed she was, heaving and wallowing through the water like a fat old girl well down in the bows. But still . . . moving.

They found out later that Captain Kelk, going below to the engine room, thought the *Southland* might stay afloat long enough for him to make a run for Lemnos and beach her at Mudros Bay.

'Is it good enough?' someone asked the chief engineer.

'I don't give it much of a chance,' he replied. 'But I've got a wife and kids, and it's good enough for me.'

As most of his crew had gone, Captain Kelk called for volunteers. Eighteen diggers – each one of whom could swim – came forward to act as stokers down in the boiler room. With the help of others who came aboard when the destroyer *Racoon* pulled alongside, the ship slowly got under way, and headed towards Lemnos, forty miles distant.

The *Racoon* wasn't the only rescue ship. An hour or so after the SOS went out, several naval vessels and the hospital ship, *Neuralia*, were in the area picking up survivors. Jim watched them draw nearer. He could make out their markings. The red cross painted over white on the *Neuralia's* hull. The sleek low lines and twin funnels of a French torpedo boat coming closer; a rope ladder down the side, and a voice calling through a megaphone:

'*Nous arrivons, mes amis!* We're coming, friends!'

'Put your backs into it boys,' said the corporal to the oarsmen. 'Give us every pound of strength you've got left.'

Jim felt the lifeboat buck and kick as the rowers ploughed through the waves towards the ship. He thought of the Greek hero, Achilles – of whom Mr Hyland had told at school – steering through the same wine-dark seas to war against Troy, on the other side of the Dardanelles. Jim thought. And then passed on. He'd ask Cec about it one day. These modern warriors had their own struggles of survival.

Willing hands and boathooks reached out to help them as they came alongside the torpedo boat. They climbed up the rope ladder, like Jacob's Dream, and onto the deck. Some men fell from exhaustion just where they were. Others wandered in a daze, taking off their life jackets and trying to recover their wits.

French sailors – the *matelots* – bustled about with dry blankets, and mugs of coffee and hot wine.

'*Allons mes amis! Du café! Du vin chaud!*'

Jim and Cec Hogan found a place in the shade on the after

deck of the torpedo boat. A French Tricolour fluttered from the stern. They sat against the ship's rail, drying out from their exposure to the sea. They were still in a state of shock, though gradually they found words to say what had happened. Bit by bit. Cec, it seemed, had been picked up not long before the lifeboat found Jim.

They were young, and a sense of normality slowly returned.

A *matelot* came up to them with more coffee and a plate of fresh bread and cold beef.

'*Mangez, mes amis!* Eat, my friends!'

The two soldier boys thought they were not hungry. But as soon as they ate the first mouthful, they realised they were ravenous. The sailor sat with them, laughing and talking away in French and broken English, as they demolished the whole plate of food. Amelia's home cooking never tasted better.

'*Fumez-vous?* You smoke? Cigarettes?'

Cec did. But his tobacco pouch was sodden and the weed useless. The *matelot* produced a whole packet of *gauloises* and matches, and joined Cec as he lit up. The lad coughed and half-choked as the strong tobacco smoke went down his throat, still rasped from sea water. But he grinned and said it did him the world of good!

'Thanks,' he said. '*Merci.*' Cec knew a little French.

'*Bien.*'

Cec tried to give the cigarettes back, but the sailor wouldn't take them.

'*Pour vous!* . . . for you. *Un cadeau* . . . a present.'

Cec hadn't anything much to give him in exchange except a copper penny, with the King's head and the legend 'Commonwealth of Australia', that he found in his pouch. It was the only thing not waterlogged.

The sailor looked at the penny and laughed. '*Australien!*' At once he removed the band from his cap and gave it to Cec. It was a black band with the name *Torpilleurs de Toulon* – Torpedo Boats of Toulon – in gold letters, with a couple of anchors. Cec kept that sailor's cap band among his souvenirs all his life.

The rescue ships stayed in the area for some time, picking up survivors, before making for Lemnos. The torpedo boat was already anchored when, later that afternoon, the *Southland* limped into Mudros Bay. Every boat in the harbour blew welcoming sirens and men lined the decks, cheering and waving, as Captain Kelk safely beached his ship.

The men rescued by the naval vessels were transferred to the hospital ship, *Neuralia*, when it reached Mudros. They were given an issue of dry clothes and a good dinner ('the best feed I ever had,' said Jim), though space was limited and they had to sleep on deck. But it was a hot night and, besides, they were so wound up nobody wanted much kip. Men lay under the rocking stars, exchanging bits of gossip. Who lived. And who died.

'Colonel Linton copped it.'

'Who?'

'The CO, dummy, of the whole brigade. Tipped out of his boat while it was being lowered, just like us. Boat fell on top of him. The poor old coot, floundering around in the water . . .

They got him aboard one of the destroyers, but he died not long after . . .'

'Many others?'

'Dunno for sure. More than thirty they say . . . fourteen of our battalion.'

'Any we know . . . ?'

'Pat Gorman of A Company . . . Dave Harris . . .'

Men that Jim Martin had known and worked with. His stomach turned over. All the sensations of drowning – of spilling deeper and deeper into the darkness – swept over him once more.

'Did you hear about the gold?' another man was saying. 'A bloke I know, one of the last off the *Southland*, told me about it . . .'

'What gold?'

'Thirty thousand pounds worth. Kept in two bullion boxes in the Paymaster's cabin.'

'Get away with you!'

'Fair dinkum. Well, after the torpedo hit us, the Adjutant, Captain Wellington, put an armed guard on the cabin with orders to shoot. But in all the barney, one of the officers came back, talked his way past the guard, and went out with his two boxes of gold. He was just about to get into one of the boats, when Captain Wellington spotted him, pulled him back, and tore the living tripes out of him. Called him a effing English bastard and no gentleman neither, taking up precious boat space with gold instead of men . . .'

'I dunno, Alf . . . He could have had *your* place next to me, with his gold. I wouldn't have minded.'

'You'd be no loss neither, digger . . .'

They all laughed.

'Thirty thousand quid, though . . . I s'pose he made them put it back . . . ?'

Later that night, one of the *Neuralia*'s lifeboats fell from the upper deck with an almighty crash!

Nobody was hurt. But everyone woke up swearing and trembling. To a man, they were sure they'd been torpedoed again.

Such was the state of their nerves.

The havoc caused by the torpedo attack on the *Southland* delayed for some days the battalion's departure to Gallipoli. Men left the ship with only the things they wore – which in some cases didn't amount to much more than a vest and a pair of pants cut off at the knees. The army had to issue new clothing and equipment, and that took some organisation.

The morning after their arrival at Mudros Bay, the survivors were transferred to the *Transylvania*. It was anchored alongside two of the world's largest liners, the *Aquitania* and *Mauritania*, now being used as hospital ships. These liners were needed to help the military hospital on Lemnos cope with the legacy of wounded from the August fighting at Gallipoli, and the rapidly rising numbers of troops crippled by disease – by typhoid and dysentery – in the summer heat.

Men of the 21st Battalion sorted themselves into their units, exchanging stories and listening with a proper sense of self-deprecation as the officers read a Special Order of the Day from the Anzac commander, General Birdwood, expressing admiration for their gallant behaviour.

'All the troops of the Army Corps have heard with pride of the courage and discipline shown at the moment when the nerves of the bravest are liable to be so highly tried,' the General said.

Which was all very well. But fine words didn't make up for the loss of so many individual treasures. Photos of wives and sweethearts, and farewell gifts. Letters from home (for those who, unlike Jim Martin, were lucky enough to get any). They didn't make up for the fact that the army didn't replace personal items like razors and combs, soap and pipes, and that the men – officers and other ranks alike – had to buy these things for themselves.

Above all, nice compliments didn't make up for the miserable food on the *Transylvania*. At Jim's table, twenty-three men had to share eighteen sausages, each no more than two inches long.

'I'd rather be back on the hospital ship,' he said. Little knowing.

On Sunday, at Church Parade, they held a service for Colonel Linton, buried now in Mudros Cemetery, and the thirty or so other personnel who had died or were missing, presumed drowned. The chaplain, Padre Stewart, received more private visits from the men in these past few days than hitherto. They were going shortly to Anzac. After the torpedo they knew they were brave and disciplined soldiers. But they also knew they were not immortal.

Equipment salvaged from the *Southland* was brought aboard. It was remarkable just how much had been saved in their kit. Cec Hogan's little book of Robbie Burns's poems. Jim Martin's paper streamer.

'I thought you lost the picture of your missus, Alf.'

'So did I, mate. But here she's turned up . . . a bit water-damaged and frayed around the edges . . . but still, large as life . . .'

'Ain't you the lucky one!'

And he was, too.

The following morning, orders came that they were to pack up again, ready for the short trip to Gallipoli. Three days' dry rations were issued. They were also given their allocation of live ammunition – ball ammunition. After months of exercising with blanks, using live bullets only at the practice range, the extra weight in their webbing pouches was surprisingly heavy. It wasn't just the bullets themselves, but the implications of all that they carried.

'It's the real thing now, Jimmy boy,' said his mate, Cec Hogan. 'Unless they drown us first.'

Images of the *Southland* still haunted the dark corners of their minds. Indeed, when the 7th Brigade arrived in harbour the next day, and the battalion was transferred to the transport *Abassieh*, life jackets had to be worn at all times.

They left Mudros Bay late that afternoon, 7 September. As they were passing the *Southland*, still beached like a whale, the old ship saluted them with blasts on her siren – and kept it up until they were well through the heads.

11: GALLIPOLI

Dusk was falling as they rounded the northern cape of Lemnos and steered for Imbros, the small island only ten miles off Anzac. Someone started to sing – a good old sing-song was becoming part of their tradition. 'It's a Long Way to Tipperary,' and 'Daisy,' and a chorus of the battalion song . . .

Yes, thrust for the old Twenty-first,
Yes, thrust for the bold Twenty-first,
With rifle and bayonet always ready
We stand as the proud Twenty-first.

Though with the gathering darkness they realised that, when next the sun rose, Turkish rifles and bayonets would also be ready to thrust against them. The singing began to peter out. Through the silence came the deep, regular boom of heavy guns.

'Battleships,' said Sergeant Trevascus, who had been in the Boer War. 'Giving old Abdul a bit of a pounding.'

'Not far then, Sarge,' said Jim, as the dark shape of Imbros slipped by on the port side. His voice trembled a little: but it was night now, and the breeze was cold off the sea.

'Not far, son,' said Bill Trevascus. He was to rise to the rank of Lieutenant and return home from France, when the war was over, with a Distinguished Conduct Medal and Bar.

All ship lights except the masthead light were doused. Closer they moved into the waters off Anzac, every eye straining and every ear alert. From time to time came the roar and flash of artillery, lighting the landmass rising before them. A destroyer near by trained its searchlight on a headland, shelling a Turkish position. A white flare exploded on the horizon and they saw, in silhouette, the cliffs and ridges of Gallipoli against the night sky.

The anchor chain ran out with a clatter. The battalion waited for the boats to take them ashore. Nobody was speaking very much. Men were smoking, alone with their own thoughts, watching and listening for this first time to the sounds of war.

From the solid darkness flashed small lights.

'They're winking just like the stars,' murmured Cec Hogan.

Moments later came a distant report!

'More like penny bungers let off at Glenferrie oval on Empire night,' replied Jim, remembering.

But then they felt movement in the air, and heard things plopping into the sea.

'What's that, Sarge?' asked Bill Hine, of A Company.

'Bullets,' replied Sergeant Trevascus, thinking of those nights on the South African veldt. 'Spent bullets from the Turkish trenches, fired over the top of our blokes and dropping down here. Watch it, though, boys. They can still do damage.'

A steam launch drew alongside. The battalion began to disembark, one unit at a time ferried ashore. It took some hours to complete. Jim's platoon was among the last to leave the *Abassieh*. It was after 0200 before they landed at the jetty – Watson's Pier – at Anzac Cove, and formed up in silence on the beach.

A guide led them past crates of ammunition and supplies, past stacks of fodder for the horses and mules, over a rise and into Shrapnel Gully leading to the ridges above. It was hard enough going in the unfamiliar darkness, without carrying the extra weight of full packs. Up and up. Shrapnel Gully became Monash Valley, named after Colonel John Monash, commanding the 4th Brigade.

Still they climbed. Until, at last, they turned into a side gully and were told they could take off their packs and rest until sun up.

Some rest! They'd hardly unrolled their blankets when along came Major Harris and said they'd all have to move again.

'Our position is rather exposed, I'm afraid. We're right in the line of fire of a Turkish machine gun.'

'Bloody hell!'

So they all moved back a hundred yards, but there was little sleep. It was all so new. So dangerous. So exhilarating. Flashes of artillery and the scream of shells bursting. Constant rifle fire, echoing so loudly down the gullies they seemed to be next to you.

Yes, and something else. Drifting on the night wind from the heights above, they smelt for the first time the stench of death. So many unburied corpses of men and animals from the August fighting lay up there, rotting in the summer heat, that the air itself was putrid. Reconnaissance pilots could smell Gallipoli from their little aeroplanes high above. Eventually, men on the ground got used to it. Or at any rate learned to live with it. But that first time, the fetid smell seeped into the very pores of their skin.

There's Death in the cup – so beware!

So sang Robert Burns in Cec Hogan's little book.

'How long before morning, Sarge, and we can have a go at those bastards?'

The same question was on the lips of every man there.

Morning came soon enough. In the grey light everyone was at Stand To, fully armed and ready for any attack that might come. It was part of the ritual of their lives, every dawn and dusk.

'Stand easy.'

The light grew stronger. Around them the rough, precipitous landscape of Anzac emerged. The steep climb up to the ochre-coloured ridges, the waterless hillsides stripped of scrubby vegetation for cooking fires. Amazing that men could fight and live there. Yet they did! Facing the sea were dugouts and pozzies scratched into the soil. They were no more than holes in the ground covered with canvas and blankets, where men cleaned and rested themselves as best they could away from the firing line.

'Home Sweet Home!'

'Welcome to Gallipoli, mate.'

The newly arrived battalions in Rest Gully had a decent enough breakfast of bacon, biscuits and tea. Then, at 0900, they marched to the tanks along the valley, filled their water-bottles, and began the hard climb upwards to their positions.

The 21st Battalion was to hold the section of the ridge from Courtney's Post on the left, occupied by D Company, Steele's Post, the lines opposite German Officers' Trench, through to A Company on the right at Wire Gully. It was a vital position protecting the head of Monash Valley. If the Turks broke through there, the main Anzac supply lines could be overrun and the whole army swept into the sea. Thus it was fiercely defended. Opposing trenches were rarely more than thirty yards apart and sometimes less than ten.

The sound of sniper fire and explosions was continuous. Every so often a shell whistled overhead to burst in a cloud of dust and shrapnel, and a man counted himself lucky his name was not on it. Soldiers lay down with their rifles. But their rest was fitful, for only the dead slept well.

The 21st was relieving the 8th Battalion, also from Victoria, which had been on Gallipoli from the beginning. As Jim's platoon was taken into the firing line above Wire Gully, they were met by a party of hardened, grimy diggers.

'What took you so long, boys? We've been waiting.'

'Waiting four friggin' months.'

'Look at youse! Smart as a regiment on King's Birthday.'

'Soon fix that.'

And indeed the soldiers were clad in very little except pants cut short at the knee, torn singlets and a wonderful variety of headgear against the sun. One bloke was even wearing a turban fashioned from his shirt. The Sar' Major at Broadmeadows would have had a fit! Only their boots were good. A man can fight naked if he has to, so long as he has a decent pair of boots.

It wasn't the diggers' clothes but their bodies that so shocked Jim Martin and his mates. Almost to a man these Anzacs were thin – shrunken, almost – as if they'd been worn down to their essential selves by months of fighting and surviving at Gallipoli. These were the same proud, young giants Jim and his dad had watched marching down Spring Street last September, reduced now by toil and battle and hard, hard rations.

And by disease. Coming up the slopes, they'd seen shadows of men, like husks, wasted with dysentery and dragging themselves between their shelters and the open latrines dug into the hillside. Men wracked with stomach pain and foul with their own ordure. Yet so tenacious in their possession of the bit of ground they'd fought for and won, they often refused to go to the medics in case they were evacuated away from their mates to the hospital ships and Heliopolis.

Liberty's in every blow
Let us do or die!

Was this what they meant by the 'Anzac spirit' that Jim so resolved to emulate? Whatever else might be said of these men, he couldn't get over his sheer admiration for what they'd achieved.

'The guts of it!' he said to Cec Hogan. They were squatting down in the firing trench as an 8th Battalion man explained the drill to their platoon commander.

'I mean, look at the slopes they rushed that first morning. Like cliffs. Turks behind every bush. Sniping. Shelling. Throwing everything at them. Yet getting to the top here. Hanging on. Beating the buggers back every time. I don't know how they did it.'

PING!

POW!

A Turkish rifle fired and a bullet skimmed the sandbag parapet of the trench.

'Christ! What was that?'

'We *did it*,' said the veteran to the new arrivals, 'by keeping our friggin' heads down, using them, and doing what we're told.'

Some idiot down the line had stuck his head over the parapet – 'just to have a look, Corp, honest,' – and nearly had it shot off.

'You're lucky Abdul's sniper over there must be green as you lot,' said the digger. 'They're pretty good. Don't usually miss.'

There were better ways of keeping watch than standing on the trench step and poking your nose over the top. Periscopes. Almost from the beginning, the tall metal tubes with mirrors top and bottom had been used for observation in the Gallipoli trenches.

Then in May a Sydney digger, Lance-Corporal Bill Beech, invented the periscope rifle. It saved countless lives.

'Come here, son,' said the 8th Battalion man to young Jim Martin. 'See how it works.'

Jim held the weapon. It was secured to a triangular wooden frame. A periscope was fixed behind the gun stock, the upper mirror raised above the level of the sandbags. Standing behind the parapet, Jim had only to look in the lower mirror to see what was happening at the Turkish trenches opposite. He steadied the rifle with his body and left hand. In his right, he held a wire attached to the trigger.

Reflected in the mirror Jim saw the broken line of country, a mere few dozen yards, between himself and the enemy's trenches. Beyond, the land fell away into the gully, before rising to the grey-green slope of the third ridge.

The rifle took some getting used to. It wasn't like peering down the sights at target practice. The weapon wavered, and it was hard at first to make sense of the reflections.

Even when he managed to hold the gun still, Jim saw no sign of activity in the Turkish trenches. Little indication that anyone was there. They might almost have strolled across and hiked up to the third ridge as if it were a Seymour route march.

There was something!

The faint movement of a khaki cap passed briefly along the trench opposite. Jim held his breath. The whole world seemed to enclose itself upon him as, for the first time in his life, he took aim at another human. He heard nothing else. Saw nothing else except the top of this head bobbing before him.

His finger tightened on the trigger wire.

Fire!

The rifle went off.

But Jim wasn't ready for the heavy recoil. He was unskilled in this kind of shooting and the shot went wide. At once, though, came a round of Turkish rifle fire in response, the bullets thudding into the sandbags, or sending up small spurts of dust where they hit the ground above the Anzac trenches.

'Hang on, Abdul!' a pained voice shouted behind them. 'The flies are still enjoying my lunch!'

'Well done, lad,' said the digger. 'You've drawn some of the bugger's fire. You'll get a lot better at it in a day or two.'

Jim's platoon stayed in the firing line for some hours, learning the lie of the land, before they were replaced and went back to get something to eat. There was a whole network – a maze – of trenches opening to the rear. Communication trenches and support trenches, only a yard wide, where men worked when they weren't on duty in the firing line. They were full of twists and turns: protection for others if a shell should hit, and better defence if the Turks should attack them.

Scraped into the earthen sides were ledges where you could rest up and eat. Like rabbits in a warren. Here they stopped that first afternoon, and opened their rations. A swig of water. A tin of bully beef, all salt and grease. And a smear of jam on biscuit.

But no sooner was food produced than swarms of flies descended upon it. Big, black flies. Hungry and dirty as sin. Millions of them. Crawling over the meat. Blowing into men's mouths as soon as they tried to eat.

'Every friggin' fly in the world has come to Gallipoli,' said the digger, spitting out half a dozen. 'Something else for youse to get acquainted with.'

Jim knew he'd swallowed some. He retched and spat.

'Don't worry too much, son,' laughed the digger. 'You can't stop 'em. You'll even find they give the bully a bit of flavour . . .'

That evening, as the sun set, the sky was bleeding red and orange over Imbros Island behind them. Again, there was no sleep. The nightly cannonade and sniper fire went on, the same as they had witnessed when they came ashore less than twenty-four hours earlier. So long ago!

At midnight, Jim's platoon was taken back to the firing line to work the shift until dawn. He peered with them into the darkness, pulling the trigger nervously in reply to each fire flash from the lines opposite, but gradually getting more confident with the periscope rifle's action and with himself. Listening to the scream of a shell overhead – ours or theirs you couldn't tell, until the explosion and the night sky lit up.

He watched and waited with his companions, talking softly with repressed elation as this first night's work came to an end. Real work. Soldiers' work. The work for which they'd enlisted those long months ago. All that remained was to claim their first kill. Their first Turk.

'I'll pot that sniping Jacko tomorrow,' Jim boasted with the rest of his section. 'You see if I don't.'

Quietly, the relief shift moved into the trench: Standing To together, as another grey dawn crept across the Gallipoli landscape from the direction of those friggin' Dardanelles they were destined never to see.

'Well, hoo-roo boys,' said the 8th Battalion men next day, as they got ready to depart. 'We're off for a little holiday on Lemnos. Give our regards to Abdul. He's all yours now, till we get back. Enjoy yourselves. You and them flies!'

They left in ragged file, down the slopes to Monash Valley and the beach and the ships that would take them from Gallipoli for an all-too-brief respite. These veterans of Anzac, some of whom had landed on that first day; who had fought with the British divisions at Helles; and held the ridge as the 1st Brigade assaulted and famously took Lone Pine, to their south, in August.

Weary and gaunt and carrying their sick, they took their leave. There was not a watching man of the relieving battalion whose heart did not go out in pride to them.

Then they turned to the task at hand. They were on their own.

Three cheers for the old Twenty-first,
Three cheers for the bold Twenty-first,
There is nothing on earth that will stop us,
Three cheers for the old Twenty-first.

12: LINE OF FIRE

So they settled to the realities of trench life.

In early autumn, things were quiet on this part of Gallipoli. Unless the brass were planning a demonstration of some kind against the Turks, the soldiers' days followed a general routine: so many hours in every twenty-four for rest, for duty in the firing line, for work in the support trenches or on fatigues. Though as always with the army, routines could change at any time.

Within the firing line, the platoon sections were divided into smaller groups of four to six men. Each group watched one narrow part of the front, for the trench didn't go more than six feet before turning a sharp, defensive corner. Two soldiers at a time generally manned the periscope and periscope rifle, the others standing by at loopholes in the parapet, weapons and bayonets at the ready, or just taking a breather. It was concentrated and tiring work – even more so when things were quiet, as at present – and a man needed regular breaks. An hour could go by without anything happening.

POW!

A single shot from a sniper's loophole.

At once the rifleman responded with a round of his own.

POW!

POW!

Then stillness once more. Silence in their own little slice of the world, whatever else was happening around them.

'Gets on your nerves, Jim, this waiting. Not knowing. Why don't they attack us? Or the brass let us have a go at *them*?'

They didn't because, after the August battles, both sides had fought themselves to a standstill. It was a matter, now, of hanging on. Of getting through the winter which would soon be upon them.

Sometimes, to relieve the monotony, opponents engaged in bomb-throwing duels: trying to lob hand-bombs and grenades into each other's trenches, where they did a lot of damage to men caught in the blast. Within days of the 21st Battalion's arrival, four men were wounded by Turkish bombs at Courtney's and Steele's.

From the start, the Turks had a steady supply of bombs from the German factories. The trouble for Abdul was that they had long fuses, which often gave the Anzacs enough time to catch the bombs and hurl them back like cricket balls. Until the Turks learned to shorten the fuses. Many diggers lost eyes and hands that way. At first, the Anzacs had no grenades of their own. In time, though, there was quite a production line on the beach, men manufacturing bombs out of old jam tins packed with bits of shrapnel, barbed wire, nails, gun cotton, a detonator – and short fuse.

On the night the 6th Brigade formally took over its section, and again six nights later, a big demonstration was held along the whole line. Artillery from the battleships and shore batteries pounded Turkish positions. Coloured flares burst in the sky. Troops in the firing line hurled jam-tin bombs and gave a burst of three rounds of rapid fire into the enemy's trenches.

The Turks responded with rifle and machine gun fire, the bullets spraying along the parapet. They'd have been deadly to any man poking up his nose. In Jim's sub-section at Wire Gully, two bombs were hurled towards the trench. They fell in no-man's-land, exploding against the sandbags and showering the men behind with dirt and stones.

'Nice try, Jacko!' they shouted in reply. 'But you're bowling 'em short, like a sheila.'

There were no casualties; but further up a man was hit when the enemy opened up on his machine gun with mortar and artillery fire. He was their first to be killed in direct action.

'You bastards!' screamed his companions seeing the bloody corpse. 'Give this to the friggin' German Kaiser! And this! And this!'

They gave him a burst of rifle fire.

One bloke had to be physically restrained by his corporal and a lieutenant from clambering over the parapet and wanting to strangle the German Emperor (had he been present on the battlefield) with his bare hands.

Strange, but already they were seeing their real enemies not as the Turkish soldiers – who were generally seen to be fair fighters – but rather their German military advisers.

'Abdul don't use exploding bullets, Jim. He don't fire on our hospital ships. And he don't use poison gas. Not like them Huns.'

When the Anzacs raised dummy human figures above their trenches to try to draw the enemy's fire, they were sometimes cut-out shapes of the German 'Kaiser Bill'. The Turks shot at such targets with pleasure. Indeed, the two sides occasionally had shooting contests, and chucked tins of food and cigarettes into each other's trenches as prizes. There were even brief moments of fraternisation: men climbing out and swapping gifts, much to the horror of Headquarters staff.

Not long after the 21st took up its responsibilities, a note written in French was flung from the Turkish lines to the men in the trenches up at Courtney's. It was wrapped around a small packet.

'We understand you lack cigarette papers,' the note said. 'We send you some.'

The boys threw them tobacco in return. They also tossed over a tin of bully beef, but Jacko threw it back. Half an hour later they were exchanging bullets again.

Strange, too, how quickly Jim – as with every soldier – got used to the constant dangers around him: how he soon slept through gunfire (though always with half an ear open), and accepted with sardonic Anzac humour the prospect of sudden death. It was a way of coping.

A week or so after their arrival, a bloke was on duty in the firing line when *Ping!* A Turkish bullet hit the swivel of his periscope rifle. The bullet was deflected downwards, passing through his eye, coming out his cheek, re-entering his shoulder and coming out again through his armpit. A medic staunched the bleeding and had the man taken down to the field ambulance, with every chance he'd pull through. The others standing around cracked a laugh.

'We always said Bert was a one-eyed coot.'

'Don't keep me too long, Doc,' said Bert as he hobbled out of the trench. 'I want to take a bet with these blokes on the chance of it happening again . . .'

A few weeks later, a shell fired from a Turkish battery landed near the dugouts shared by Jim's platoon. It exploded just as they were walking to the rest terraces after their second shift. The men were knocked off their feet by the force of the blast.

Jim felt a shard of metal whiz past his cheek. Another inch or two . . .

'That was a close shave, Sarge.'

'Close enough, lad,' said Sergeant Coates. 'You won't need to use your razor tonight.'

Some joke. They'd spent the shift helping the sappers dig a tunnel – a sap – deep underground, beneath the Turkish trenches. The engineers filled the mine with explosives and detonated them at the right time.

Boom! And suddenly it was raining dirt, and barbed wire, and bits of Turk.

They even dug saps under their own trenches, just in case the enemy over-ran them and could be blown up. Both sides went in for mining, especially up at Lone Pine where the 23rd and 24th Battalions relieved each other every two days. Cec Hogan had a couple of mates up there – Benalla boys, with the home town inked on their hat bands. They spent much of their time digging. It was said to be one reason the Anzacs called themselves 'diggers' in the first place. The *tap-tap-tap* of people digging away under you was one of the sounds you got used to in the trenches. And you were never quite sure if they were our sappers or *theirs*!

Like every digger, Jim found it hard, dangerous and dirty work, lying for hours on his stomach, burrowing away like a ferret with always the risk of a cave-in. The men came off the shift covered in muck, with hardly any water to wash themselves. And here was a shrapnel shell exploding outside the rest terraces and Sergeant Coates saying, 'You won't need to use your razor tonight . . .'

No one, thank God, was seriously hurt in the blast. Nor were they when a shell burst near Church Parade one Sunday.

'You must have been praying extra hard that time, padre.'

They were not always so lucky.

One afternoon, Jim and Cec were on water fatigues. In the summer heat, acute water shortages were one more hardship endured by the Anzacs on Gallipoli. There were few wells, and they were mostly dry. The good water was on Abdul's side of the line. Little rain fell. The Anzacs had to bring in clean water for drinking and washing by barges from Lemnos and sometimes even from Egypt, and pump it into storage tanks at Anzac Cove.

Each day a water detail had to make the trip down Monash Valley to the beach carrying kerosene tins, fill them with precious water, and carry them back up the slopes to the trenches. It was a risky job, exposed in the open to artillery. But then, nowhere was safe at Gallipoli – and water duties were a break from trench routine. Sometimes you could even nick down to the sea for a quick swim. It was a rare chance to get your clothes off and wash your whole body – even if you did have to share the seawater with mules and shipping, with oil slicks and lively bursts of shell fire from the Turkish battery known as 'Beachy Bill'.

On this particular afternoon, the water party was returning up the valley carrying the laden kerosene tins. From time to time came the sullen thud of a Turkish gun over the ridge. Above them, they heard a German biplane buzzing, a black iron cross painted beneath its wings. The pilot was manoeuvring to drop a bomb on the Anzac lines. Ahead of them, beside the track, a group of diggers were standing in a ring playing two-up.

'Head 'em up!' they cried, as the spinner got ready to toss the pennies. 'Head 'em up again!'

A second buzzing sound could be heard. The water party looked up and saw a British aeroplane flying across the sky, like a large insect, to intercept the German. They stopped and put down their tins to watch the fight. The two-up game took no notice.

'All bets on?'

'Come in, spinner!'

The pennies spun in the air. The German pilot spotted his enemy and quickly changed course.

KKKRUMPPP!!

There was a terrific explosion. A shell had landed just beside the two-up game. When the dust cleared and Jim raised his head, only half the game were still standing. Four men lay dead on the ground, and a fifth was screaming.

'Oh no, God! Oh, please mother! Not me guts! Not me friggin' guts . . . !'

The soldier's prayer. Anything, except shot in the stomach. The wound was usually fatal. And death was slow and agonising.

The water party ran across. A head, like a discarded football, lay in the dirt. The man nearest the shell had been blown to pieces, his limbs scattered into the scrub. Blood dripped everywhere, attracting hosts of Gallipoli flies. The screaming soldier held his stomach, to stop his intestines spilling onto the ground.

'Oh, sweet Jesus, not that . . . not me guts . . .'

There was a field ambulance station near by in Rest Gully. Someone ran to get help, but the stretcher bearers had heard the explosion and were already on their way.

The soldier, as they carried him down, found enough strength to cry out, 'Tell the missus . . . tell me kid . . .'

He was fortunate, in a sense. He died quickly that afternoon on the operating table in the Red Cross tent, and was buried with his mates in the little cemetery by the beach.

'Poor old Hughie,' said the spinner of the two-up game. 'His luck was just starting to change, too.'

'We should send his winnings to his missus.'

'Double 'em or nothing . . . ?'

'Nah . . . We should send 'em.'

The water party picked up their kerosene tins and began the hard climb back up the hill to Wire Gully.

The water they carried was more than precious. It was everything. Sure, it always had a faint taste of kerosene, and sometimes men got by with only two cups a day. But with that half pint of water they had to cook their food, sponge themselves, shave, clean their teeth and – with luck – have enough left over to wash a pair of socks. It could be done, with practice. It all depended on the order in which you did it!

Even so, as the excitement of the first week on Gallipoli gave way to acceptance and even monotony, disease began to make its presence felt. Men came down with high temperatures and fevers. Symptoms of diarrhoea and dysentery appeared at the daily sick parades, especially among the reinforcements. Nine days after they arrived Cec Hogan went down to the Casualty Clearing Hospital with a bad attack of diarrhoea. He was kept there for four days before being sent back to duty.

The battalion Medical Officer, making his report, observed that many of the sick had defective teeth, one important way by which infection could enter the body. But the problem was very soon not confined to the reinforcements. By late September, the Adjutant was noting in the battalion diary that four officers and eighty-three other ranks had been sent to hospital, of whom twenty-four were injured, most of them accidentally. The rest – over sixty men – were sick.

Partly it was the poor diet – that disgusting mix of tinned bully beef, an occasional bit of cheese or bacon, and hard biscuit ground into porridge or spread with a little jam. Rarely was there fresh bread, meat or vegetables.

'We are not doing bad for food,' Jim Martin wrote home a few weeks later. But he was just telling them what he thought they'd want to hear. In truth, the food was such it was no wonder a man's strength was weakened and his constitution sapped by disease.

Partly, too, it was vermin. The CO was strict about hygiene. No food or liquid was to be left uncovered. The latrine pits were well away from the sleeping dugouts. Soldiers on fatigue duty daily swept the trenches for every bit of litter and rubbish.

'Mother would be proud of the clean-as-a-new-pin-like appearance of our trenches,' Captain Gordon Maxfield told his parents in a letter home, 'even if she was not altogether proud of the grimy and bearded inhabitants.'

But the best housekeeping in the world couldn't keep fleas and lice out of trenches, and out of men's hair, and out of men's clothes. Every day, when he came off duty, the first thing Jim did was have an 'insect hunt': going through his clothing, piece by piece, picking out lice and fleas. It was why men grabbed any chance for a swim in the sea, whatever the risks.

The most rigorous sanitary precautions couldn't keep away rats either. It didn't matter if every scrap of food was covered. There was much else for them to eat in the bloated and decaying corpses that lay unburied on no-man's-land between the trenches. Turk and Anzac alike.

Even the buried dead were not left undisturbed. Every so often, diggers mining underground broke into an unmarked grave. The rotting corpse, crawling with maggots, provided another feast for the vermin and flies which had grown fat in the hot autumn weather from the dead, the dunnies, and the food men tried to get into their mouths.

Not surprising that one in twenty of the battalion's strength were sick, after only three weeks. The figure would rise to nearly eight in every twenty by the time they left Gallipoli in December.

For the time being, though, these things didn't seem to greatly affect young Jim Martin. The soldier boy still had his strength. He still had his mates. He was still doing what he wanted. 'Don't worry about me,' he wrote home on 4 October, 'as I am doing splendid over here.'

That day, the troops received a special treat, courtesy of Lady Ferguson, the Governor-General's wife: two fancy biscuits, a half stick of chocolate and a couple of sardines each. Life was full. If anything, Jim was becoming a little bored with the long periods of inactivity on the front. Whole days went by when the Adjutant noted in the battalion diary, 'Nothing of importance happened.'

So it was with this Private up at Wire Gully. 'It is very quiet where we are,' he wrote to his mother and father, 'so we are not seeing much of the fun. Now and again we give a few rounds rapid fire and the artillery and the mountain batteries, the torpedo boats and cruisers send a few extra shells in. Then we get them to waste there ammution' (his pencil was slipping on the regulation army letter paper) 'for about twice as long.'

Indeed, he told them, 'We have not had many casualties yet. There has only been one poor fellow of our old company been shot and killed and two or three wounded . . .'

No. There was only one thing that pained Jim Martin, and it cut the lad to his heart. He still had received no letters from his family or anyone at home. A mail arrived from Australia in mid-September, but once again there was nothing for him.

He tried to be brave about it. But it was no good. 'It is very dishearting to see all the others getting letters from home,' he wrote, struggling with the words, 'and me not even getting one. I have not received any since I left Melbourne on June 28th. So they must be going astray somewhere. I hope you are getting some of mine as I am writing pretty often . . .'

Just as he promised he would, when they let him go.

Jim asked after them all. Aunt Mary and Bill Musgrave at Maldon. Remembering his sisters', Mary and Annie's, birthdays. Hoping the house in Mary Street was full of boarders and the fowls laying plenty of eggs. 'How is Mary and Annie and Millie getting on at school and tell them all to write. Is Alice still at home?'

Not knowing that Alice had married Percy Chaplin, the military policeman, in August. Not knowing that the whole family *was* writing to him all the time. Not knowing where or why their letters were being lost . . .

'I remain Your loving son, Jim.'

He scribbled a postscript at the top of the page. 'Write soon as every letter is welcome here.'

13 : DEATH

Three days after Jim wrote this letter, the weather began to turn. Battleships had just finished bombarding Turkish positions to the south, towards Lone Pine, when a great storm blew in. The wind was like a hurricane and rain fell in torrents. Men were flushed out, trying to sleep in their dugouts, and the trenches ran like creeks.

It was the first sign of approaching winter, something that was worrying military minds at Gallipoli. At Brigade Headquarters, orders were prepared for support troops to start digging deeper shelters against the frost and snow that would come sooner or later.

Already the days were turning cool. One morning they woke to see a heavy fog hanging in the gullies and over the sea, the cloud tops tinged with pink in the rising sun. As with the glorious sunsets they still sometimes saw, nature had a caprice of painting backdrops of rare beauty against which men acted out their tragedy.

More chill winds blew.

Cec Hogan took sick again on 5 October, and went down to the Casualty Clearing Hospital near the beach. The lingering infection was giving him severe muscle pains in his back and limbs; and the doctors kept him there for a week to recover from myalgia, before sending him back up the line on duty.

His mate, though, continued in good health.

'Dear Mother and Father,' Jim wrote from his dugout on Saturday, 9 October. 'Just a line hoping all is well as it leaves me at present. Things are just the same here. The only difference we are expecting a bit of rain which will not be welcomed by us. This place will be a mud hole when the rain does come. We had a bit of a shower last night, but it was nothing to speak of . . .'

The cold was being felt by men of both sides, of course. Jim went on to tell them at home of reports from a Turkish officer who had surrendered to the Anzacs. The Turks were being very badly treated by their German advisers, he said, and were only getting one meal a day – in the evening.

This officer wasn't alone.

'There was one Turk who tried to give himself up the other night,' Jim wrote, 'and got shot by the sentry. We dragged him into our trenches to bury him in the morning, and you ought to have seen the state he was in. He had no boots on, an old pair of trousers all patched, and an old coat. The pioneers took him down the gully to bury him, and one got shot in the thigh by a sniper . . .'

It was the first time Jim had seen his Turkish enemy close up: face to face, one human being to another. He was an older man, with sons of his own, no doubt. Bearded and dirty, his face shrunken and showing all the surprise of unexpected death, the name of *Allah* still half-uttered on his cold lips. Jim looked with equanimity upon this man's corpse. However young, Jim had seen death before, and it came to them all eventually.

'We are not doing bad for food,' Jim said in his letter, telling Mum what she'd want to hear. White lies for home consumption. And he went on to tell Amelia and Dad about the treat from Lady Ferguson. But it was cold, and he was tired, and he was getting to the end of the page.

'I think I have told you all the news so I must draw to a close with Fondest love to all, Jim.'

Again, he scribbled the familiar postscript. 'Write soon, Jim. I have received no letters since I left Victoria and I have been writing often.'

He made another copy of the letter, filling in a few gaps, before putting it in the battalion post to be read and passed by the military censors. It would seem that this was his last.

The soldier boy lying so ill with typhoid on board the hospital ship *Glenart Castle*, anchored out there off Anzac, stirred fitfully in his slumbers.

He was dying.

The images began to fade. It seemed, in these past few minutes, he'd lived again all that had happened since they had left Port Melbourne in June. Now, like a silent picture show when the projector breaks down, the light in his mind started to flicker and waver. His consciousness began to stall and wind down. The scenes became slower, more broken and distant, until, at length, there were only fragments of memory sputtering in the darkness, and the rest of the screen was blank.

Jim Martin's heart, weakened by fever, beat ever more feebly. His blood, poisoned with typhoid bacteria, pumped more slowly through the veins and arteries and into his darkening brain. The morphine had helped. But not enough. His nervous system and bodily organs, one by one, were shutting down.

Yet Jim was still young. Only fourteen. And soothed by the motion of the ship lying at anchor, life and mind sought briefly once more to assert themselves.

It wasn't long after writing this last letter that Jim Martin began to feel sick. Nothing serious at first. Just a feeling of lethargy in his arms and legs when he woke one morning. A few aches and pains. Things had been very quiet all along the front for some days. Perhaps he was getting used to it. Growing a bit soft.

Yet the feeling of malaise persisted. A dull, throbbing headache started and wouldn't go away. He began to cough. A dry, hacking cough, like bronchitis.

'Are you all right?' asked his mate, Cec Hogan. Cec was not long back from his week in the Casualty Clearing Hospital, and was alert to other people's symptoms.

'Right as rain. Just a bit cold.'

'Good-oh.'

But Jim wasn't all right. His coughing got worse. His nose bled once or twice for no reason. And although his stomach began to ache, his bowels seized up. He'd go down to the latrines and squat on the boards over the pit, reeking of filth. Yet nothing would happen.

'You sure you're not crook?'

'Just a few pains . . . like you had.'

'You oughta see the medics . . .'

'Look! I'll get over it! Just like you did.'

'Keep your shirt on! I'm only saying . . .'

Cec was standing next to Jim in the firing line. It was 0400, and the brigade was giving Abdul another demonstration. Artillery boomed. Rounds of rapid fire were directed up and down the line. Dummy figures were raised above the parapets, the men cheering and officers shouting bogus orders.

'First assault party, mount the firing step!' As if they were about to launch an attack on the Turkish trenches.

But Abdul didn't respond in his usual way. The demonstration drew little enemy fire. It was as if he knew it was just a demonstration, without serious intent, and his heart was not in it.

Nor was Jim Martin's. Standing in the trench, he found it hard to make much sense of what was going on or what he was supposed to be doing. His gut ached. He couldn't hold the rifle steady. He shouted as they were told, but all that came out was vomit.

'Are you *sure* you're not crook?'

'I told you! I'll be all right.'

'I'm only trying to help.'

'Then leave me alone . . .'

A mail from Australia arrived the next day. Cec got a letter from his sister, Kath. He wrote his reply that very afternoon, having a rest from digging mines.

Once again, it appeared, there were no letters for Jim Martin. He could no longer hide his disappointment. That night, in the privacy of his dugout burrow, tears welled up in Jim's eyes. What were they doing? Why didn't they write? He was putting the correct return address on his own letters.

Gallipoli
1553 A Coy 21st Bat.
6th Brigade

What was the matter with them? Things were so unfair. From a long way off, Jim heard his words again to his mother and father in the kitchen at Forres.

'If you let me go, I'll write to you and stay in touch. But if you don't, I'll run away and join up under another name, and you won't hear from me at all.'

Well, he'd written to them almost every week. Now, as it

turned out, it seemed *they* weren't writing to him!

It rained for most of the night. But Jim woke up feeling hot and feverish. He was ill again that day on duty, and the following day as well.

'You should report to sick parade, Private.'

'I'll be all right Sergeant Coates. It will pass.'

Though it didn't pass. In the second week of sickness, Jim's fever rose. The cramps in his stomach got worse, until it seemed as if the pain was eating through him. He could hardly drag himself along the sap. And in the trench, when it was his turn to man the periscope, he had trouble focusing upon the image in the mirror. He wasn't always sure where he was.

Sometimes in the fractured light it seemed he was back at Tocumwal . . . or was it the practice range at school . . . ? No . . . surely those brown and olive hills were the landscape around Maldon . . . ?

POW!

A bullet rang out.

What was that? Where did it come from? Were they out rabbiting? Trying to pull his mind back . . .

'Bit slow responding there, Private! Sharpen yourself up.'

'Yes, Corporal. Sorry Corp.'

As if from a great distance.

A day or two later the dysentery started. His bowels, cramped and constipated before, let loose. Jim could scarcely haul himself to the latrines before he seemed to void half his innards down the pit. Every half hour or so the searing pain returned, until it was easier to lie wrapped in his blanket and his own faeces on a groundsheet by the dunnies than go back to his dugout; until the cold and rain returned in the third week of October and drove him underground. Then he was like one of the 8th Battalion shadows he'd seen shuffling to and fro that first day they came up to Wire Gully. And like them, he refused to go down. Tenacious in his refusal to surrender anything.

> *May coward shame distain his name*
> *The wretch that dares not die.*

Jim Martin was no coward.

'Jim, you've got to go to the medic!' Cec Hogan pleaded with him. 'You're crook. Real crook.'

'No. I told you . . .'

'There's no shame in it, mate. No one will think any the worse of you. *I* got sick. Twice. I went down to the tent hospital. They fixed me up good, and sent me back . . .'

'I'll be all right I reckon. Just some water . . .'

His throat burned.

Jim's water-flask was empty. Cec unscrewed his own and held it to his friend's lips. Yet as soon as Jim took a swig of the precious water, he spewed it up again. He could keep nothing down, and nothing would quench the fires inside.

The next day he could scarcely move when it was time to get up for duty.

'Jim, you've got to report to sick parade. You've got to see someone . . .'

'Please. No. Just tell Sergeant Coates . . .'

'But why, mate? Why?'

How could Jim Martin say why? How could he say that deep down, beneath a soldier's bravery and chosen duty, lay dread? His dread that if he did go down to the doctors they'd soon discover his true age. They'd *see* he was just a boy. And what then? He'd be stripped of everything by the army, and sent home in disgrace.

No shame? How could Cec Hogan know that? They were both under-age. But Cec didn't know how young Jim really was.

'I'll be right as rain tomorrow.'

But he wasn't. He lay sweating and shivering by turns, tormented by thirst and calling for water. He couldn't sleep for the pain in his gut, and night became indistinguishable from day.

Fear came. Not just fear he'd be found out. But also fear that perhaps he might *not* be all right. Fear that he might die. As others had died. The whitened face of the drowned steward from the *Southland*, his head wound seeping blood, rolled in the waves of Jim's fevered consciousness. The terrified eyes of the cabin boys sank beneath the sea.

Jim tried to pray, as he had been taught.

Our Father which art in Heaven . . .

Or was it *who art . . .* ?

He couldn't remember or shape the words. For the dead Turk watched as they dragged him down the gully for burial, calling on *his* God. And from afar, Jim heard the agonies of the two-up player, clutching his guts and crying:

Tell the missus . . . tell me kid . . .

Thoughts of home came into Jim's mind. Of his bedroom at Forres when he was sick with a cold, and Amelia coming up the stairs with a basin of hot balsam . . . Mum bending over him and soothing his brow with such soft hands and words . . .

Gentle Jesus, meek and mild . . .

The night-time prayer from his childhood.

Until Jim pushed all such thoughts away. Forcing them to leave him alone, because he would not – he could not – give in.

That evening, Sergeant Coates came to see him.

'You're a good lad, and a brave one. But unless you're better tomorrow I'll send you down to the doctors whether you like it or not. We don't want to lose you.'

So on that next cold, quiet day, 25 October, Jim made himself join the platoon in the firing line at midday. He was thin and pallid, and had lost almost half his body weight. His head throbbed and his gut ached to hell, though he said he was fit for duty.

He stood with his section in the raw afternoon. The light shifted and ebbed along the ridge line, as though it were already dusk. Shaking.

'How are you feeling now, Jim?' asked Cec Hogan.

'Not too bad.'

'I could do with a hot brew myself,' said Cec's mate from Benalla, Bob Briggs. 'You want something?'

Rest Gully, where the 6th Brigade had breakfast before the hard climb up to their positions. [AWM C01477]

Home sweet home. Dugouts behind the ridge at Wire Gully – holes in the ground covered with canvas. [AWM G01077]

The periscope rifle – better
than poking your head over
the top. [AWM H10324]

A risky job – water carriers
with their kerosene tins full of
precious cargo.
[AWM G01241]

Quite a production line making tin-can bombs: jam tins packed with shrapnel, barbed wire, nails, gun cotton, a detonator – and a short fuse.

[AWM H10291]

The horror of war – burying the dead on the truce of 24 May 1915.

[AWM H03954]

Percy and Alice Chaplin with their two sons,
James Martin (left) and William Glen (front).
Behind (from left to right) are Millie, Mary, Esther
and Annie. [Courtesy members of Jim Martin's family]

Cec Hogan's engraved brass shell where he wrote
the names of his closest mates, second among
them J. Martin. [Courtesy Cec Hogan (son)]

Water. Just some water.

The voices receding and disappearing as the pain burst again from his inner darkness.

'Mum . . .'

This time Private Martin wanted only to go home.

He collapsed on the floor of the trench. Excrement and blood and vomit flowed from his body.

He lost all consciousness.

They took Jim by stretcher down the hill, down to the ambulance station in Rest Gully. He was far gone; and the medical officer, after only one look, knew that he had to get to hospital and have proper care immediately if he was to be saved.

'Do what you can for him. Clean him up a bit. Give him some water. Then move him at once to the beach and put him on the first transport available out to the hospital ships.'

So Jim was carried down to Anzac Cove and laid in an open barge that was taking that day's cargo of sick and wounded soldiers to the *Glenart Castle*, anchored offshore. Far more sick than wounded. With the coming of cold weather, the swarms of Gallipoli flies with their arsenal of disease had begun to disappear. But for many soldiers it was too late.

Thus the barge was towed out to the hospital ship and Jim Martin, in his turn, was lifted aboard by the orderlies and taken down to the crowded ward. His filthy clothes, once so new and proudly put on, were cut away. His wasted body was sponged clean. He lay in a bed and the first cool sheets he'd known for months.

'Water . . . please, water . . .'

A nurse helped him drink – such sweet water – and gave him an injection of morphine to help ease the pain.

Jim lay there, borne upon the tide. Images of home and of himself floated on the slow currents of his mind. The river at Tocumwal, eddying past the sandbanks . . . *rat-a-tat, rat-a-tat*, the drum beating as Mary and Annie hurried the last few steps to school, hair ribbons flying . . . the faces of those boys as they marched down Spring Street that day he stood and watched with his father . . . *If you let me go, I'll write to you and stay in touch . . .*

'Please . . . more water . . .'

Calling weakly. And then the woman's face, with a voice like his mother, from out of the misty veil.

'Am I going to get well . . . ?'

'Of course you are, my boy . . .'

So that was all right. Right as rain.

'Thank you, sister. I feel better already.'

Jim Martin settled down. Comforted. The ship rocking. Was it the *Berrima* . . . the *Southland* . . . the *Abassieh* . . . carrying him to new and distant lands?

He felt himself slipping through the waves. The paper streamers, red-and-white, breaking one by one. No longer holding him to shore . . .

The currents flowing.

Slowing.
Gathering in pools of darkness.
And silence.
Mum . . .
Ever deeper.
And slower.

Then nothing.

14: AFTERWARDS

The morning after Jim died, Matron Reddock sat down to write her letter of condolence to his mother.

Dear Mrs Martin,

Before this reaches you, you will have already heard of your very sad loss in the death of your son. I thought you might like a few lines from me as I was with him for the very short time he was on this boat.

He was brought on board from the shore yesterday at 5 p.m. in a very collapsed state. We got him to bed comfortably and did everything possible for him. He said he was feeling much more comfortable and thanked me *so* nicely for what had been done for him. He then settled down to get a sleep but died quite suddenly and quietly of heart failure at 6.40 p.m . . . He will be buried at sea . . .

Frances Reddock enclosed something she found among his papers, though what it was became forgotten over time. A photograph? A last letter to Amelia? Possibly the first version of Jim's letter of 9 October, for two different copies survived in his boyish handwriting. The military records said letters were found among Jim's effects, but the family memory remained clear: he received none of the letters that were sent to him.

The rest of Jim's 'little treasures' as Matron Reddock called them – his New Testament, a notebook, the aluminium dog tag with his battalion number on it and his name crudely scratched, his belt and pouch with the paper streamer – were done up in a parcel and eventually sent home to Mary Street through the regimental office.

Nine days after Jim's body slipped beneath the Aegean Sea, his mate, Cec Hogan, wrote to Amelia.

Dear Madam,

I am writing to you on behalf of the old No 10 Tent party to express our great sorrow at your late bereavement.

Jim was in the firing line with us and he took bad. But he stuck to his post till the last like the brave lad he was and made the greatest and noblest of sacrifices for his Country. Sargt Coates of his platoon No 4 speakes very highly of him, and says he never had a man in his platoon who paid more attention to his duty.

I am yours faithfully, Cecil Joseph Hogan.

The local Member of Parliament, Mr W.M. McPherson, wrote to Charlie and Amelia to express sincere sympathy and public sentiments.

Australia is proud of the spirit of self-sacrifice that prompted our men to come forward in the Empire's hour of trial, and to give up their lives in upholding Britain's Just Cause and in defending our National Honour.

Of course there was the military telegram at the beginning of November, informing the family of Jim's death. It was followed by a letter dated 16 November, three days after Annie's birthday, advising formally that Private Martin of the 21st Battalion had died of syncope (low blood pressure due to heart failure) following enteritis (the term they used for typhoid).

Nowhere in these letters was there any indication the authorities – or even his closest mates – knew Jim's true age. They may have guessed he wasn't quite eighteen. There was the hint of it in Cec Hogan's letter. He only turned seventeen himself on the day Jim was buried. But fourteen? It was a secret Jim Martin seemed to have kept to himself until the end.

Strangely, though, the fact that this soldier boy was probably the youngest of all the Anzacs was put on the public record within two months of his death.

On Saturday, 18 December 1915, the Melbourne *Herald* newspaper published a photograph of Jim Martin in his slouch hat beneath the heading:

YOUNGEST SOLDIER DIES

It is believed that Private James Martin, who died of enteric while on active service, was the youngest soldier in the Australian forces.

Though the regulation provides that the minimum age shall be 18, Private Martin is said to have been only 14 years of age when he enlisted. He was the only son of Mr and Mrs C. Martin of 'Forres', Mary Street, Hawthorn, and was on board the transport 'Southland' when that vessel was torpedoed. He was rescued after having been in a ship's boat for several hours.

For some reason – possibly military embarrassment – the authorities censored news of the *Southland* for over two months. It wasn't until late November that reports and photographs of the torpedo attack appeared in the Melbourne newspapers. Six days before Jim's story appeared, the *Herald* published a photograph of the ship and a statement by the 21st Battalion's CO, Lieutenant Colonel Hutchinson. 'It was a remarkable sight to see the steadiness of the men. It was a grand sight. I never felt prouder of the boys.'

In their grief at the news of Jim's death, the family made it known that he, too, had been on the *Southland*. Clearly, from the report that Jim had spent some hours in a ship's boat, he'd written to them describing his experience. But, like much else, this letter would not apparently survive. In an interview, many years later, Jim's last living sister, Annie (Mrs Nan Johnson), recalled that he'd spent four hours *in* the water, and expressed the family's belief that this was what weakened him. Annie remembered the mourning of that time: of the news coinciding with her own tenth birthday, and of Amelia's hair turning white overnight from shock.

Two days after Jim's story appeared in the newspaper, his sister Alice gave birth to her first child, a son. She and her husband, Percy, named the baby after the dead soldier boy: James Martin Chaplin.

Remarkably, on that same day, 20 December 1915, the last of the Australian and New Zealand troops left Gallipoli. Headquarters was becoming alarmed by the severity of the winter, with men already suffering frostbite and some even freezing to death. Cec Hogan was one of those who had a bad case of frostbite and trench feet. By curious coincidence, he was taken aboard the *Glenart Castle* on 7 December and evacuated to the

1st Auxiliary Hospital at 'Luna Park', Heliopolis, where he and Jim had visited those sick and wounded diggers a few months before.

Convinced also by the weather and the military futility of hanging on, the British Government decided to evacuate Gallipoli. Between late November and 18 December, the Allied forces were gradually reduced to 20,000 men each at Anzac and Suvla. They were then taken off the peninsula over the next two nights.

Elaborate stratagems were devised to fool the Turks into believing the army was still present in force. There were long periods of inactivity to get the enemy used to silence. Men played cricket on Shell Green. Battleships bombarded Turkish positions. Men rigged devices to keep their rifles firing at intervals. But stealthily in the night, their boots wrapped in hessian, the Anzacs filed down to the beach and into the waiting boats. Just after 0400 on 20 December the last boat left Anzac. The remaining British troops at Suvla departed an hour later. The Turks attacked that day – to find the trenches empty and the invaders gone.

The evacuation was a masterpiece of planning. While quantities of stores and ammunition were left behind or destroyed, some 80,000 men, 5000 horses and 200 guns were taken off this part of the peninsula. High Command had reckoned on losing half the troops in the operation. In fact there were only half a dozen casualties. The following month, Allied troops at Cape Helles were also withdrawn at negligible cost in human life.

It was often said that if the *invasion* of Gallipoli had been planned with the same care and attention as the withdrawal, the campaign could have been won within a week. As it was, there were over 33,000 Allied dead and 78,000 wounded. Of these men and boys, there were over 8700 Australians and 2500 New Zealanders killed, and more than 19,000 Australians and 5000 New Zealanders sick and wounded. Turkish casualties were estimated at over 200,000.

Not all the sick died, of course. Unlike Jim Martin, many soldiers recovered at hospitals in Egypt or England, and rejoined their units to fight in Palestine or France. Cec Hogan was one of them. During the Gallipoli campaign itself some soldiers were sent back, too soon and unfit, to the trenches. Others were invalided home to Australia, their war over. But Jim's death, not in some heroic feat of battle but rather killed by flies and the infection they carried, was all too typical of what the medical historian of Australia in the Great War, Dr A.G. Butler, who was there himself, called the 'disease debacle' of Gallipoli. During September and October alone, some 50,000 Allied casualties were evacuated through Mudros Bay. Of these men, 44,000 – almost nine out of every ten – were sick.

Insufficient fresh food, little water for drinking and washing, dirty eating utensils, heat, fatigue, unburied corpses, vermin, sick men returned to the lines, dysentery – above all, flies and the lack of fly-proof seats in the latrines during summer – were compelling factors.

'Black swarms of flies carried infection warm from the very

bowel to the food as it passed the lips . . .' Butler wrote. 'Sticking it out against disease was made a point of honour; it was, indeed, accepted by the corps commander as the official policy. A man was evacuated only when he was no longer of use or had some blatant contagion.' By which time it was often too late.

Some 220 men of Jim Martin's battalion were among the last of the troops to leave Anzac on 20 December 1915. They were taken to Lemnos, and then back to Egypt. From there the 21st Battalion went to the Western Front, where it fought with great distinction and valour as part of the Australian Imperial Force throughout the rest of the war. It was the first Australian infantry unit to serve in the front line in France. It was the last AIF infantry unit in the line before the Great War ended with the Armistice at 1100 hours on 11 November 1918. Remembrance Day.

While the true figure would never be known, it was esti-mated that over eight-and-a-half million soldiers from both sides were killed in the war, and another twenty-one million wounded. Interestingly, in February 1918, nine months before the Armistice, the hospital ship *Glenart Castle* was itself torpedoed by a German submarine in the Bristol Channel. There were no sick on board, but more than 150 nurses, medical officers and crew drowned. Matron Reddock was not among them. After Gallipoli she was embroiled in a dispute over staff and discipline, and her contract as a military nurse was not renewed. She returned to England in September 1916 and died in June 1919, aged only forty-three.

Altogether, nearly 60,000 Australian soldiers were killed in the Great War. Jim Martin's mate, Cec Hogan, survived the slaughter, and returned to Australia in March 1919. He was gassed in France, nearly died from double pneumonia, and was there when they tried to amalgamate the 21st Battalion, reduced to a few hundred men, with other battalions of the 6th Brigade. The men flatly refused to obey the order – though subsequently, in the last weeks of the war, they became part of the 24th Battalion.

While he was at Nalinnes, in Belgium, waiting to return home, Cec engraved a brass shell case as a 'Souvenir of the World War.' The quality of his workmanship was remarkably fine. Around the top he included reminders of Egypt: a sphinx, a pyramid, the crescent moon and star, and Arabic writing. On one side, Cec engraved a shield surrounded by the Australian and New Zealand flags, with the Rising Sun badge of the AIF, two boomerangs and a kookaburra. The shield was surmounted by a kangaroo, the words 'Egypt, Anzac, S.S. Southland, Belgium, France' in a ribbon, and the 21st Battalion's red-and-black diamond colour patch. There was a cannon and shell beneath, with the motto *Aut. Pace. Aut. Bello.* (Either In Peace Or In War). On the other side of the shell case, Cec engraved the letters R.I.P. And in a scroll he wrote the names of six close mates who had died. Second among them was J. Martin.

Cec came home to Benalla, on the same day as his mate, Bob Briggs; and while he didn't become an architect (though his son, Cec, did), he was a skilled builder and designer in the Albury district. He supervised the construction of the Regent Theatre in Albury, eventually listed with the National Trust. Cec married in 1925 and had three children. And when the Second World War broke out in 1939, Sergeant Hogan enlisted again to serve in Australia, among other things as a guard at Prisoner of War camps. He died at Albury in 1951, at the age of 53.

For the Martin family, life ran its uncertain course through sunlight and shadow.

Jim's sisters married and had families of their own. Esther had two sons and another daughter, Millicent ('Billie'), who years later would help make Jim's story more widely known. Alice had a second son, William Glen, born in 1917. Mary married John Harris in 1921. They had two sons, John (Jack) and Robert. Amelia married Frederick Bullock in 1934, and they had one daughter, Nancy. Annie married Albert Johnson in 1939, but they had no children.

The bond of kinship between the sisters and their families was a close one, united by the affection and strong personality of their mother, Amelia. Visiting, sharing, helping Amelia in her businesses. Keeping the memory of their dead brother alive. Talking about Jim to their own children, though less so as time went by. It was in the past. Still, Amelia gave some of his photographs and letters to her daughters. She gave them his service decorations, too, when they arrived after the war: the 1915 Star, the British

War Medal, the Victory Medal, the Memorial Plaque and a Memorial Scroll from King George himself:

> He whom this scroll commemorates was numbered among those who, at the call of King and Country, left all that was dear to them, endured hardness, faced danger, and finally passed out of the sight of men by the path of duty and self-sacrifice, giving up their own lives that others might live in freedom. Let those who come after see to it that his name be not forgotten.

As it turned out, it was well that these things were shared among the family.

Charlie and Amelia continued to live at the boarding house in Mary Street until 1921. By 1922 or 1923 they had separated. Doubtless there were many reasons, but inevitably there must have been recrimination – even guilt – that they'd let their soldier boy go to war. If only they'd been stronger, whatever Jim's threat to run away . . . If only they'd meant it when they'd said no . . . If only they'd made sure the authorities discovered Jim's true age . . . The catalogue of 'if only's' would have been endless.

Charlie Martin still drove his taxi, waiting for fares outside Camberwell railway station. He saw the family from time to time, though feelings could be strained. Charlie paid Amelia some support money and helped her with odd jobs. For Amelia continued to let rooms in various places around Hawthorn until, in 1927, she returned to Mary Street and took on another boarding house. Two years later she moved back to Forres, which she ran in conjunction with the Maryemeade boarding house next door. In 1930 yet a third establishment, just around the corner, was added to her business.

It was hard work, and the family was often called in to assist. Not surprisingly, Amelia soon relinquished the leases. Instead, she took over a weekend chalet at the outer suburb of Park Orchards, and a little later became proprietress of the Hartwood guest house and picnic grounds at Mitcham.

Then in October 1933, Charlie Martin died of kidney failure. It was the first of a number of misfortunes to afflict the family.

Less than a month afterwards, the Mitcham guest house burned to the ground. Alice and Annie were sleeping in the same room as Amelia when they woke to find the weatherboard house on fire. They escaped with little more than their nightclothes. Annie ran half a mile to telephone, but when the fire brigades arrived the place was a ruin. A photograph appeared in the *Herald* on 20 November, and the report said Amelia had lost £150 worth of furniture and nearly all her other private possessions representing her life savings. Among them, it would seem, were some of the letters and photographs Jim had sent from the war.

In August 1934, Alice's eldest son, James Martin Chaplin, named after Jim, also died. He was only eighteen. The lad was an epileptic. He belonged to a military cadet training unit and, tragically, shot himself at home with his service rifle.

So passed the years.

Amelia returned to Melbourne after the fire. She was fondly known to her grandchildren as 'Ma Martin', for she often stayed with one or other of her daughters until her death in 1955 at the age of 77. In the following decades Esther, Alice, Mary and Millie passed on, until Annie was the only sister still alive. Although Jim Martin's name was inscribed on the Roll of Honour at the Australian War Memorial in Canberra and at the Lone Pine Cemetery and Memorial, it seemed his story might soon fade from memory.

It didn't. In 1982 Esther's daughter, Billie, began to research Jim's life. Two of her own grandsons, Stephen and Ian Cruwys, were joining the Army Reserve, and she wanted to tell them of their great uncle, the youngest of all the Anzacs. Documents, letters, photographs and medals were gathered together. Jim's last living sister, Annie (Mrs Nan Johnson) spoke of him to the newspapers. The family decided to give the material to the Australian War Memorial in Canberra. On 25 October 1985, the seventieth anniversary of his death, a service and exhibition was held to honour Jim's memory. Twenty members of his family were present.

In the years to follow, the story of Private James Martin would be recounted to numerous schoolchildren visiting the Gallipoli galleries at the War Memorial. His photograph would be published in Anzac histories. Jim Martin would become part of the nation's story. In 1999 his name would be singled out for mention by the Governor-General of Australia, Sir William Deane, at the Anzac Day service at Lone Pine . . .

The morning light slants across the rugged peninsula of Gallipoli. It's a strong light, just as it is at home, throwing into high relief the cliffs and ravines leading up to the ridges. The landscape is softer than the Anzacs knew, for wild thyme and rosemary, the low scrub, scarlet poppies and Aleppo pines have grown again. Indeed, it is dedicated by the Government of Turkey as the Gallipoli Peace Park. Even so, when the bushfires go through, you can still see the trenches of Anzac exposed like scars in the burned earth.

From the Lone Pine Memorial you look down to the blue Aegean Sea and marvel at how far those first Anzacs had come. You look up and realise how far they had to go. Here at the cemetery are buried men who died throughout the campaign, from the beginning to the end, the known and the unknown.

'Here too,' the Governor-General is saying on this April morning, 'are commemorated over 4200 Australians and 700 New Zealand soldiers who have no identified grave or who were buried at sea. Among them Private James Martin, who died on a hospital ship. He was, we believe, only fourteen – though he said he was eighteen – perhaps the youngest of all the Anzacs to die here . . .'

His words are caught by the wind and carried away. Across the ridges above Wire Gully. Blowing down the slopes and paths they called Monash Valley and Shrapnel Gully. Over the stones and sand of the beach, and out to sea where the hospital ships once lay at anchor.

So fresh and alive in the spring morning! The wind is whispering new words now, once spoken by Kemal Atatürk, the Turkish commander at Gallipoli and first President of the Republic. Words that are there for all of us on the memorial at Anzac Cove: 'You, the mothers, who sent their sons from far away countries, wipe away your tears. Your sons are now lying in our bosom and are in peace. After having lost their lives on this land they have become our sons as well.'

Appendix I

JIM MARTIN'S LETTERS HOME
(A WM Collections PR 83/061 and PR 85/339, except as noted)
(Grammar, punctuation and spelling as written)

Military Camp Broadmeadows
Salvation Army Tent
26/5/15
1st Rein. 21st Batt.

Dear Mum & Dad

Just a line hoping all is well as it leaves me at present. I seen about those photos this evening. He had sent them to the wrong Martin. We got news this evening to say that the camp is going to be sifted to Seamore. But I don't think we will go as we are expecting to go any time now. It is still pretty muddy out here yet. I think I have told you all the news. Hoping all are keeping well.

> I remain
> Your Fond Son
> J Martin.
> I will be out any time now but I don't know when. Jim.

★

Seymour
21/6/15

Dear Mum & Dad

Just a few lines hoping all is well as it leaves me at present. We are not sailing Monday now but think we will be going either Wednesday or Monday. I am sending you a couple of Groups of six of our tent today. The road up here is no better than Broadmeadows in fact it is a lot worse it is just like soup. There were a few people up here on Sunday but not as many as we expected. I caught the 6.35 train from town on Saturday night arrived here about 9.30 and they did not know I had been away so I am as wright as rain. It is raining all the time up here. I went to the railway station for that parcel but could not get it that night. I think I have told you all the news so I must draw a close. Give my love to all.

> I remain your loving son
> Jim.

★

Military Camp, Seymour
Salvation Army Tent
Seymour 24/6/1915

Dear Mum & Dad

Just a few lines hoping all is well as it leaves me at present. I have just received that underclothing now. I would have sent you a wire on Monday that we did not go on Monday but the Post Office will not let us send them saying when we are going so I could not send it. We are told we are going Monday now for certain. We could not go before until we had completed our shooting. We were down the Range on Tuesday and Wednesday shooting and I passed my Musketry. We are having plenty of rain up here. I am sending a couple more photos again and one to Aunt Mary. I think I have told you all the news so I must draw to a close. Give my love to all.

I remain
Your loving Son
Jim.

*

Heliopolis
Thurs. Aug. 26th

Dear Mum & Dad

Just a few lines hoping all is well as it leaves me at present. I have not been here long enough to get a return from one of my letters. I have been going pretty solid this last fortnight as we have had some hard work to do before we leave for the "Dardanelles" as we are going tomorrow Friday 27th August to the Dardanelles to have our share of the Turks. I think [*the word 'hope' is scratched out*] I will be well in it by the time you get this letter. We are packing up now. Did you get that couple of handkerchiefs for you and Dad and that centre & a couple a dozen scenes that I gave Albert to give you. I will try & write as much as I can over there. There is nothing to tell you as everything is Desert and work so I must draw to a close with best love to Essie & Charlie & Essie [*their daughter*], Alice, ?, Mary, Annie and little Mill and Dad & Mum. Remember me to Aunt Mary & Annie & Bill & George. Xxxxxxxxx

I remain

Your loving Jim

[*on side of letter*]

Many happy returns to Mary & Alice's & Mum's Birthdays & be sure to write soon

★

Gallipolli

4th October

Dear Mother & Father

Just a few lines hoping all is well as it leaves me at present. Things are just the same here. The Turks are still about 70 yards away from us. We have not had many casualties yet there has only been one poor fellow of our old company been shot and killed and two or three wounded. It is very dishearting to see all the others getting letters from home and me not even getting one. I have not received any since I left Melbourne on June 28th. So they must be going astray somewhere. I hope you are getting some of mine as I am writing pretty often. We have been in the trenches about a month now so we are more used to it. It is very quiet where we are so we are not seeing much of the fun. Now and again we give a few rounds rapid fire and the Artillery and the Mountain Batteries the Torpedo boats and Cruisers send a few extra shells in then we get them to waste there ammution for about twice as long. I hope your house full up with boarders and the fowls laying. How is Mary & Annie & Millie getting on at school and tell them all to write. Is Alice still at home. How are Essie, Charlie and babie. Is dad and yourself in good health and remember me to Aunt Mary & Annie and George & Bill all the rest. Wish Mary & Annie a many happy returns of the day for me. Don't worry about me as I am doing splendid over here. I have told you all the news so I will draw to a close

I remain

(Your Loving Son Jim)

[*At top of letter*]

Write soon as every letter is welcome here.

[*The letter is marked 'Passed by N Wellington' – the same officer who was Adjutant on board the troopship* Southland.]

★

Gallipoli
1553 A Coy 21st Bat.
6th Brigade
Sat. 9th Oct. 15

Dear Mother & Father

Just a line hoping all is well as it leaves me at present. Things are just the same here. The only difference we are expecting a bit of rain which will be not welcomed by us. This place will be a mud hole when the rain does come. We had a bit of a shower last night but it was nothing to speak of.

Occording to an account of a Turkish Officer who gave himself up the other night says that the Turks are getting very badly treated by the German officers and are only getting one meal a day and that was in the evening. There was one Turk who tried to give himself up the other night and got shot by the sentry. We dragged him into our trenches to bury him in the morning and you ought to have seen the state he was in. He had no boots on, an old pair of trousers all patched and an old coat. The pioneers took him down the gully to bury him and one got shot in the thigh by a sniper in the Turks trenches. We are not doing bad for food we got that little present from Lady Ferguson [*wife of the Governor-General*] that was 2 fancybiscuits 1 half stick of chocolate and 2 sardines each. I think I have told you all the news so I must draw to a close with Fondest love to all

I remain your loving son

Jim

[*On top of letter*]

Write soon Jim

I have received no letters since I left Victoria and I have been writing often.

[*There are two versions of this letter. This copy has been passed and signed by A Robertson – Captain Robertson of Headquarters staff.*]

★

LETTER FROM
MATRON FRANCES HOPE LOGIE REDDOCK

H.M. Hospital Ship
Union-Castle Line
S.S. "Glenart Castle"

26. 10. 15

Dear Mrs Martin

Before this reaches you, you will have already heard of your very sad loss in the death of your son. I thought you might like a few lines from me as I was with him for the very short time he was on this boat. He was brought on board from the shore yesterday at 5 p.m. in a very collapsed state. We got him to bed comfortably and did everything possible for him, & he said he was feeling much more comfortable & thanked me *so* nicely for what had been done for him. He then settled down to get a sleep but died quite suddenly & quietly of heart failure at 6.40 p.m. That was yesterday, 25th October. He will be buried at sea. I found the enclosed amongst his papers. The remainder of his little treasures that were in his pockets I have done up in a little parcel which will be sent through the regimental office, with anything else of his there may have been that did not come with him.

I know what a terrible grief it is to you to lose him, but you must I am sure feel very proud of him for so nobly coming forward to fight for his country.

Yours in all deep sympathy
(Mrs) Fr H.L. Reddock
Matron

★

LETTER FROM PRIVATE C.J. HOGAN

Anzac
Gallipoli
Nov. 5th 15

To Mrs Martin

Dear Madam

I am writing to you on behalf of the old No 10 Tent party to express our great sorrow at your late bereavement. Jim was in the firing line with us & he took bad but he stuck to his post till the last like the brave lad he was & made the greatest and noblest of sacrifices for his Country. Sargt Coates of his platoon No 4.

speakes very highly of him & says he never had a man in his platoon who paid more attention to his duty.

I am

Yours Faithfully

Cecil Joseph Hogan

★

LETTER FROM CEC HOGAN TO HIS SISTER
(Private Collection)

In the Trenches

Anzac, Gallipoli

Oct 17th

Dear Kath

I received your most welcome letter this morning & was very glad to know that you got the card alright. Bob and I are still together. Ross Thompson & Russian Harvey wish to be remembered to you. It is very cold here at present. I don't think it will be too long now before we will be back as I think Mr John Turk is just about sick of it they often come & give themselves up. You ought to see them when our batteries stick the Lydite into them you can see Turks & barbed wire in the air like a shower of rain. Willie Stewart is over here now in the 24 Batt. I see there has been nothing about us being torpedoed yet, in the papers. We are not too far from the sea here, so we often get a chance of a wash but at present I haven't had a wash or my clothes off for about a week. Beachy Bill likes to tune us up with shrapnel while we are swimming but we are getting too quick for him now so he doesn't do too much damage. Fancy Dougie Gallagher coming over here too. The lads give all the guns (big guns) names for instance there is Whistling Rufus, Sneaking Sal, Tired Tim, Beachy Bill, Annie, & dozens of other names. We don't see too much of the Turks here as we all fire through the loopholes. Our chaps sap right under the Turks trenches & then blow them up. I am in a tunnel under the Turks at present. It seems funny so near to them & yet they don't know. Well Kath Dear I can't give you any more news at present as it is getting dark. Remember me to Uncle & Auntie & Dorrie & the boys. I would write to Bessie only I forgot her surname.

I am

Your loving brother

Cecil

(excuse scribble)

APPENDIX II

EXTRACT FROM THE SUN-HERALD
22 APRIL 1984
(Reprinted by kind permission)

'NEVER MIND DAD'
The youngest Aussie ever to go to war
By Graham Gambie

Jim Martin, a strapping 6ft boy just out of short pants, went to war because his father had been rejected as medically unfit.

'Jim said, "Never mind Dad, I'll go",' said Mrs Nancy Johnson, 78, the last remaining member of Private Martin's family, last week.

And she still cries with the memory of an incredibly touching moment.

'My mother was so much against it – she said he was only a boy – but Jim said "If you don't allow me, I'll run away and join under another name."

'So mother let him go, thinking he'd get sick of it and come home or that they'd find out he was only 14 and not send him away.

'But he went on board the *Southland* to Gallipoli, which was torpedoed and he was in the water for four hours – that's what weakened him – and he died of enteric fever.'

Mrs Johnson said she believed several boys of 15 joined the Army at the same time as her brother, but as she pointed out: Jim didn't live to be 15.

'There was a notice in the old newspaper, the Melbourne *Argus*, which said he was the youngest soldier ever,' she said.

'One thing I do remember was that my mother said the recruiting officers said Jim was the fittest specimen they had in that day.

'I was only nine at the time and most of my memories were of him in short pants although my parents bought him a pair of longies because he was so big, he was taller than our father.'

The story of Private Martin, which has waited nearly 70 years to be told publicly, came to light when his niece, Mrs Wilma Carlton, of Minto in Sydney's outer western suburbs, discovered that two of her six grandchildren were going to join the Army Reserve.

She told them about their distant relative and one of them commented immediately, 'he looks like a baby.'

As she looked at the collection of souvenirs, photographs, letters and a copper medal that she had collected in the past two years, Mrs Carlton said, 'There's not much left for a life is there – being only 14 when he died, he never really got started.

'But as my grandson said to me, "It shows that even if our Aussie image is painted everywhere as just Ockers, we've still got a lot of brave guys."

'When you see the photo of the young boys who went with Jim, they didn't look like the military at all.

'They just look like young boys who have been put through their paces, learned how to fire a gun, got thrown into uniform and shipped off.

'I've got a 17-year-old grandson as well, who has put in his application to join the Army, but if you said to him, "Come on, slip the gun on and off you go" – he'd have a fit.'

After collecting all the records from the baptism certificate to the record of Private Martin's grave at Lone Pine Cemetery at Gallipoli, Mrs Carlton and the family decided to give his money belt, his dog tag and his belt to the Australian War Memorial in Canberra.

An official letter from the Curator of records says the items will be housed in the Library and Relics Section for research and possible display . . .

APPENDIX III

21st BATTALION, A.I.F.
6th INFANTRY BRIGADE

BATTALION SONG

There's a Flag proudly floats o'er the ocean,
'Tis the flag of the Southern Cross so free;
It fills all our hearts with emotion,
We've followed it across the mighty sea.
We'll plant it on the battlefields of Europe,
And on our trenches it will be flying first,
By the blood of our boys we will uphold it –
Here's luck to the old Twenty-first!

Here's luck to the old Twenty-first,
Here's luck to the bold Twenty-first,
For the flag of our country will float higher
When held by the proud Twenty-first.

Now then let's toast the King, boys, God bless him,
We'll soon have fresh lands for him to rule,
No longer the German oppressor
Our loyal sons of Austral Land will fool.
There's a war-worn old Kaiser and an Empire,
And upon them will all our fury burst,
We will think of our little Belgian comrades,
And thrust for the old Twenty-first.

Yes, thrust for the old Twenty-first,
Yes thrust for the bold Twenty-first,
With rifle and bayonet always ready
We stand as the proud Twenty-first.

For our Colonel's a man that we're proud of
And we've got a good Second-in-command,
The Adjutant keeps us all working,
And everyone appreciates our Band.
In drill we can stand above all others,
All the Germans and Turks can do their worst,
But there's nothing will daunt our brave Australians –
Three cheers for the old Twenty-first.

Three cheers for the old Twenty-first,
Three cheers for the bold Twenty-first,
There is nothing on earth that will stop us
Three cheers for the old Twenty-first.

(Printed on letterhead of the 'SS Ulysses'. In the Williams Collection, AWM PR 91/113. Ivor Williams notes in his diary it was sung for the first time at a concert on 3 June 1915, as the battalion passed into the Red Sea. He doesn't give the tune.)

ACKNOWLEDGEMENTS

Many people have helped me with information, advice, and access to material during my research into the life of Jim Martin and while writing this book. I express my thanks to each of them, although naturally the responsibility for any errors of omission, commission or interpretation of the facts is mine alone.

In particular, I again acknowledge the generosity and guidance of members of Jim's family: Mr Jack Harris, Mrs Nancy Cameron, and Mr Stephen Chaplin; and also of Mr Cec Hogan, the son of Jim's wartime friend. Each made photographs, letters and family recollections available, and gave permission to print them. I thank them deeply.

I am very grateful to the Director and Staff of the Australian War Memorial in Canberra – Mr Ashley Ekins, Senior Historian, who first drew my attention to Jim Martin's story and kindly shared his knowledge with me; the curators, members of the Education Section and the Research Centre – for all their help. I acknowledge the kind permission given to reprint photographs in the Memorial's collections.

I thank the Department of Defence for permission to reprint the Rising Sun badge on the chapter headings of the book; and the *Sun-Herald* for permission to reprint Graham Gambie's 1984 article on Jim Martin.

I appreciate the help given by the Director and Staff of the National Library of Australia, particularly at the Reference Desk and in the Newspaper and Microform Room.

I also acknowledge the kindness and help I received from Anne Nevins, Berrigan Shire Librarian, Cr Elizabeth McLaurin, Mrs Margaret Ballhause, Mrs Elaine Bate and Mrs Lynne George, all of Tocumwal; Mr James Logan, archivist, Charles Sturt University Regional Archives; Registry of Births, Deaths and Marriages in Victoria and NSW; National Archives of Australia; the Department of Veterans' Affairs; staff of the Victorian Public Records Office; Mrs June Healey, the Returned & Services League of Australia, and Central Army Records Office, who gave advice on tracing returned servicemen; staff of the Public Records Office, London.

I thank the Boroondara City Library for assistance with Hawthorn municipal records; Gwen McWilliam, for generously sharing her knowledge of Hawthorn local history; the Principal, Mr Geoff Burt, and staff of Glenferrie School 1508; General Sir Phillip Bennett; Mrs Elizabeth Burness, formerly with the AWM

Education Section; Dr Chris Coulthard-Clark; Dr Alan Cowan, who gave valuable medical advice; Sir William Deane, who gave me much encouragement and support; Rev Tom Frame; Margaret Francis, for permission to photograph James Martin's former residence; Rev Rod Gallagher; the late Colonel Reg Gardner; Hon Bill Hayden, with whom I visited Gallipoli in 1995 as a member of his staff; my daughter, Jane Hill, for research at the State Library of Victoria; Mrs Nadia Kuhlmann; my friend, Dr Michael McKernan, who advised on many aspects of military history and kindly read the manuscript; Lieutenant Colonel Neil Smith, whose history of the 21st Battalion has been an important source of information.

I also wish to acknowledge the assistance I received from my friend, Don Barnby, and members of the Australian Army when I first had the idea for a war book some years ago: the Director of Army Public Relations, Queensland; the Commandant of the Land Warfare Centre, Canungra, Queensland; Lieutenant Colonel Rod Webster, who also kindly read the manuscript, and members of 5th/6th Battalion, Royal Victoria Regiment; the Commandant, Staff and Officer Cadets of Royal Military College of Australia, Duntroon.

I was privileged to visit Mr Roy Longmore, among the last of all the Anzacs. Mr Longmore served at Gallipoli in Jim Martin's battalion, and speaking to him gave this book a living presence. I thank him and his son, Mr Eric Longmore, who made my visit possible.

Finally, I mention my great uncle, Mr Vernon Waring, of

Melbourne. Late in the writing I discovered that his brother (and consequently also my great uncle), Howard, served in the 21st Battalion and in the same Company at Gallipoli as James Martin. Like Jim, Howard did not return from the war, and I know that his family never ceased to mourn him. Thus do our many connections with the past resonate into present and future lives.

Anthony Hill

REFERENCES AND FURTHER READING

Adam-Smith, Patsy, *The Anzacs* (Penguin, Melbourne, 1991)

AIF War Diary, 21st Bn, September–December 1915, AWM 4 microfilm roll 54.

Armstrong, Lt Donald, 21st Bn, letters 1915, AWM 1DRL/0057. Lt Armstrong was killed in France in October 1917.

Barnes, Sgt B., 21st Bn, B Coy, letter September 1915, AWM 2DRL/0004.

Barrett, John, *Falling In, Australians and 'Boy Conscription' 1911–1915* (Hale & Iremonger, Sydney, 1979).

Bean, C.E.W., *Anzac to Amiens* (Australian War Memorial, Canberra, 1983). See pp 61 and 84 for boy sailors on *HMAS Sydney* and at the Gallipoli landing. Boys on *Sydney* were 16–17 years old, Jose *qv.*

Bean, C.E.W., *Official History of Australia in the War of 1914–18,* Vols I & II, *The Story of ANZAC* (Angus & Robertson, Sydney, 1938). See Vol II pp 807–809 for the *Southland.*

Bell, Pte Alexander, 1st Reinforcements 2lst Bn, diary begins at Suez, July 1915, AWM 3DRL/1307. Alex Bell, 29, was killed in France in August 1916.

Butler, Col A.G., *Official History of the Australian Army Medical Services in the War of 1914–18.* Vol I (AWM, Melbourne, 1938). See pp 249, 364, 376 on Gallipoli's 'disease debacle'. Ibid, Vol III, AWM, Melbourne, 1943, see pp 371 and 493 for use of morphia.

Currie, Cpl Albert and Pte Will, private letters 1915-1916, describing the voyage from Australia to Egypt. The Tocumwal brothers were both killed during the war.

Dennis, Peter *et al. The Oxford Companion to Australian Military History* (Oxford, Melbourne). See pp 174–175 for boy cadets 1911–1922.

Embarkation Rolls, 21st Bn, 1st and 2nd Reinforcements, AWM 8 fiche 1077–1082.

Gammage, Bill, *The Broken Years* (Penguin, Melbourne, 1975).

Garvey, Stella, *Stella,* in *Yesterday's Daughters*, Alma Bushell (ed), (Nelson, Melbourne, 1986). Cec Hogan's sister tells of growing up at Greta and Benalla, Cec going to war and his homecoming.

Goodman, Rupert, *Hospital Ships*, (Boolarong Publications, Brisbane, 1992).

Hine, Pte William Lionel, 21st Bn, A Coy, diary on arrival at Anzac quoted in Smith *qv.* Bill Hine, who rose to the rank of sergeant, died of wounds in France in August 1916.

Hogan, C.J., private letter to his sister, Kath, from Gallipoli, 17 October, 1915. See also Martin collection for condolence letter.

Jose, Arthur W., *Official History,* Vol IX *The Royal Australian Navy,* (Angus & Robertson, Sydney, 1937). See pp 186-7 for training ship boys in the *Sydney–Emden* fight.

Laffin, John, *Gallipoli* (Kangaroo Press, Sydney, 1999).

MacNeil, Capt A.R. MC (ed), *The Story of the Twenty-First* (21st Bn Association, Melbourne 1920) reprinted 1971.

McWilliam, Gwen, *A School for Hawthorn* (Glenferrie Primary School 1508, Melbourne, 1975).

Martin, Pte James, private letter and letters in the AWM Collections, AWM PR 83/061 and PR 85/339, including the condolence letters from Cec Hogan and Matron Reddock.

Maxfield, Capt Gordon Loris MC, 21st Bn, letters 1915, AWM 1DRL/0489. Captain Maxfield was killed in France in May 1917.

Odgers, George, *The Royal Australian Navy, An Illustrated History* (Child & Henry Australia, Brookvale, 1982). See p 41 for cadet midshipmen beginning naval training at 13–14 years.

Reddock, Matron Frances Hope Logie (nee Hogarth), see under Martin, James, and also her file with the Queen Alexandra's Imperial Military Nursing Service at the Public

Records Office, London, WO 399 6903. Born in Wales,
Frances Reddock spent some time nursing in India. Her
husband was Captain John Reddock, who commanded a
troopship in the Great War.

Registry of Births, Deaths and Marriages, Victoria and NSW.

Robertson, John, *Anzac and Empire* (Hamlyn Australia,
Melbourne, 1990).

Sands NSW Directory, 1900–1914.

Sands & McDougall's Directories for Victoria, 1909–1930.

Scott, Ernest, *Official History*, Vol XI *Australia During the
War* (Angus & Robertson, 1938). See p 439 on lowering
recruitment standards during the war.

Smith, N.C., *The Red and Black Diamond, The History of the 21st
Battalion 1915–1918* (Mostly Unsung Military History,
Gardenvale, 1997).

The Australian Encyclopedia (Grolier, Sydney, 1981).

The Argus, Melbourne, August–September 1914,
March–November 1915.

The Herald, Melbourne, March–December 1915, 20 November
1933.

The School Paper, Education Department Victoria, monthly
editions for Grades VII & VIII, 1913, 1914, 1915.

Wellington, Capt N.F. MC, 21st Bn, Report on the torpedoing
of SS 'Southland', AWM 3DRL/3509.

Williams, Cpl Ivor, 21st Bn, diary May–December 1915, AWM
PR 91/113. Ivor Williams kept a very detailed, descriptive
and helpful diary of his war experience. He returned to

Australia in 1918, served in the Second World War, and died in 1975.

PHOTOGRAPHIC CREDITS

Every effort has been made to trace copyright holders of photographs. The publishers would appreciate hearing from any copyright holder not here acknowledged.

FRONT COVER AND SPINE: Photograph of James Martin courtesy of Australian War Memorial, Canberra (Australian War Memorial negative number P0069/01). Photograph of sunset over the Sphinx at Gallipoli, 1995, © Suzanne Wilson. Crest courtesy Australian War Memorial, Canberra.

BACK COVER
Photographs of Jim Martin and Amelia Martin courtesy members of Jim Martin's family – Jack Harris, Nancy Cameron, Stephen Chaplin.

INSIDE FRONT COVER
Photograph of Jim Martin courtesy members of Jim Martin's family.

INSIDE BACK COVER
Memorial Scroll courtesy Australian War Memorial, Canberra.

AUTHOR PHOTOGRAPH: copyright © Sandy Spiers.
WAR MEMORIAL PLAQUE: courtesy Glenferrie Primary School, Hawthorn, Victoria. Photograph by Suzanne Wilson.

PICTURE INSERTS

The following photos are from the Australian War Memorial Photographic Collections: AWM A02740; AWM H15309; photograph of Jim Martin's surviving possessions donated to the AWM by Jim Martin's family – courtesy AWM; AWM J00352; AWM J00320; AWM PO858/08; AWM PO2226.022; AWM H16957; AWM H12827; AWM A00742; AWM C01477; AWM G01077; AWM H10324; AWM G01241; AWM H10291; AWM H03954.

OTHER PHOTO CREDITS

Jim's maternal grandmother Frances Smith – courtesy members of Jim Martin's family – Jack Harris, Nancy Cameron, Stephen Chaplin.

The Tocumwal store c. 1895 – courtesy Elaine Bate and Lynne George, Tocumwal.

Forres, Mary Street, Hawthorn – courtesy Margaret Francis. Photograph by Suzanne Wilson.

Jim with his five sisters, 1915 – courtesy members of Jim Martin's family.

Charlie and Amelia in the garden at Forres – courtesy members of Jim Martin's family.

Men on the *Southland* – courtesy Elaine Bate and Lynne George, Tocumwal.

Cec Hogan – courtesy of Cec Hogan's son, Cec Hogan.

Percy and Alice Chaplin with family – courtesy members of Jim Martin's family.

Cec Hogan's engraved shell – courtesy Cec Hogan's son, Cec Hogan.